My Brothers

My Brothers

Jordynn W

For more information, contact:
rice4299@outlook.com

FIRST EDITION

978-1-80541-468-1 (paperback)
978-1-80541-469-8 (ebook)

This short story is dedicated to all of us who have scars in our life. We won't forget about them, but we can still live with them. Always believe we are still blessed and the life is worth to fight with.

PART ONE

I

Twelve years ago

Joshua sat on the floor with his back against the sofa, staring at the Peter Rabbit jigsaw puzzles absent-mindedly. His hand held several pieces, but apparently, he was not going to look for the vacancies they fit in front of him. He was usually a patient little boy, but today he could not wait. He wanted to go out for a big dinner with his family.

He turned and gave a glance to his twin sister beside him. She had the same short natural chestnut hair as him, with two shallow dimples on her angelic jelly cheeks. She was now giving her full attention to the puzzles. Joey was only ten minutes younger than him, his mum told him before. Unlike some other children who became jealous and tried to get more attention from their parents, Joshua was completely different. He beat other children who made fun of Joey and he always shared his snacks with Joey even if they were his favourite chocolate cookies.

It was their seventh birthday today. Their mum bought them two blue jackets and two pairs of new leather shoes as gifts after they got addicted to the story of Peter Rabbit, and they would eat out tonight. Everything sounded perfect. But it seemed their parents had got stuck with an unpredicted visitor in the living room for more than thirty minutes.

"Do you have other pieces for his ears?" Joey's voice suddenly called out from the silence of their bedroom. She had almost finished the puzzles, but now she was pretty sure her brother held the last three or four pieces in his hand.

"Oh, sorry, here you are."

"Wow, yay! Look, now it's perfect. Here we go." She squinted with a bright smile with her long eyelashes covering her eyes. Now she began to feel starving.

"Are you hungry?" Joshua asked, and then grabbed some cookies for her. He knew his sister very well.

"Daddy and Mummy are still talking?"

"Yeah... I don't know the man they're talking with. But Mummy seems not very happy."

"Why? I hate him. What does he look like?"

"I didn't see him. I only heard his voice, very deep, and seems like he came here to find Daddy. But when I asked Mummy for our puzzle, her face was pale and she just asked me to stay in our bedroom."

Joey did not respond to her brother, and her smile disappeared. How could that annoying man upset their mummy and ruin their birthday? Would he hurt them?

"Don't worry, I'll protect you." Joshua put his arm around his sister's shoulder gently. "Maybe they'll come to us after…"

He stopped because his mother pushed the door of their bedroom suddenly without knocking. She had never done that before. Her hands were trembling, and they heard the fuzzy sound of quarrelling and struggling from the living room. Something was off.

She shut their bedroom door without any hesitation and grabbed her children to the corner of the room.

"What's wrong, Mum? Where's Daddy?" Pure fear was seen in the eyes of the children.

"My boy, be quiet now please. Listen to every word I say." She bent down and pulled her children in front of her, breathing heavily. "You know your bedroom can be locked inside, don't you? Lock it at once and don't open it until I come back, you hear?"

Joshua was scared by his mother's words. He realised something was wrong, and he knew his mother was not joking anymore. She talked really fast, without any gap. Without saying yes, his tears came out. "Mummy…"

"Tell me you're listening to my words, Joshua." She was shaking her son's shoulder and lowering her voice. "And you too, Joey. Keep silent. You can't make any sound. Joshua, you're the brother, the boy, you know how to protect your sister, don't you? Promise me, please."

There were still tears inside his eyes, but he nodded firmly without hesitation.

Joey was sobbing.

"Okay. God bless my children..." She held them in her arms and hugged and kissed them for a few seconds. Then she turned around and left.

The kids heard their mother's footsteps vanishing in the corridor. A few seconds later, they heard their mother's voice again. But this time she was crying, begging and there was extra noise outside.

Bang. Bang. Bang.

Joey burst into tears and could not help opening the door.

"No, Joey, no... close the door!"

Joey was frozen when she saw the view in front of her.

At the end of the corridor, there was a masked man standing there with something heavy in his hand, and he kept hitting their mother who was already lying on the floor.

Joshua pulled his sister back into the bedroom before the man turned around. He quickly locked the door from inside and covered her mouth with his hand.

Then they heard footsteps again. Closer to their bedroom. Of course, it was not their mother. The one outside the door was the most horrible monster.

Click. Click.

The door handle moved, but then stilled. Silence. Were they now safe? Joey held her brother's waist from behind his back. She tried not to tremble, but it did not work. Was their mum okay? Where was their dad? Who was that man?

They heard the bang again. Outside the door. He was trying to break in.

Joshua removed his sister's hands from his waist.

"Oh my God, what should I do now?" he said to himself.

They had to hide. At least he had to hide Joey first. But where? There weren't many choices. There was some space under the bed and the windowsill covered by the blue curtain. The security window stopped them from escaping outside. What else? The wardrobe? No way. Every time he played hide-and-seek with Joey, he would be found by Joey at once if he stayed there. The man would be clever enough to find out.

There was a bang again. This time much stronger. Time was running out.

Suddenly, he noticed a huge trolley case filled with thick clothes under the bed. These were prepared in advance to get ready for the winter. He poured the clothes on the floor, pushed his sister into the case and made a shush gesture to face the fearful expression in the eyes of his sister. If Joey did not make any sound, she might be safe. He had done his most important job. The last step was to lock the suitcase.

Bang. The doorframe was gone.

Joshua had no other choice. He had no time to lock the suitcase. He closed the zip rapidly and opened the wardrobe. Just after he closed it, the bedroom door fell completely.

His heart seemed to stop beating. But after one second, he became unbelievably calm. He even opened the wardrobe to try to see the man's face.

And then he saw him. The man turned his back to him.

He was very tall, dressed in black with a pair of black boots. Joshua could not identify anything familiar about him, but there was a little sculpture in his gloved hand which belonged to his dad.

There was blood.

The guy looked around, and then slowly bent down to look under the bed with a purely evil smile. No one was there. He even took out the big suitcase under the bed and kicked it several times.

Both twins covered their mouth with their hands. The air was freezing.

Suddenly, the man turned around and looked at the wardrobe. Joshua quickly looked away and curled into a ball in the corner. But the heavy footsteps did not come to the wardrobe.

What is he doing? Joshua thought, but he did not dare look through the crack. He was scared the guy was staring through the crack into the wardrobe. Maybe he would open the wardrobe and kill him. He held his breath and closed his eyes.

What he expected did not happen. Instead, he heard the footsteps move away from the side of the wardrobe.

Now he could not wait. Did he find Joey? Joshua stood a bit and looked from the crack again. This glance made him almost scream. The man was looking under the bed, taking out the suitcase.

No, please don't! Just leave her there! He could feel his hand trembling, but he held his hand over his mouth to stop himself making any noise.

Although Joey did not make a sound, she would be found in a few seconds. Damn! What could he do?

Joshua did not notice his tears flowing. He knew he had already made his decision. He remembered his last promise to his mother.

"You know how to protect your sister, don't you? Promise me, please." Her voice was full of tenderness, but he would not hear it anymore.

The bedroom door was just beside the wardrobe. If he was fast enough, he could go to the front door of the house to ask for help. In that case, Joey would be safe again. That would work.

Joshua rushed towards the front door without turning around until his leg was gripped behind him.

The man dragged the struggling boy back to the bedroom without any mercy. The boy's hand was even trying to hold the floor tightly to resist being dragged. He tried to kick the man's knee to make him lose balance, but it did not work.

Silence again. The man smiled. Finally, it was time for him to clean up the mess he had made, from the living room to the bedroom.

But just then, the doorbell rang.

2

Joey

I am woken up by thunder. It is bucketing down at midnight. The rain hitting against the roof has lasted for more than two hours, with a squall whipping the freezing air. A few seconds later, a flash of lightning appears in the dark sky.

Boom.

I almost jump out of my quilt. What did I see? In the dark. The only faint light comes from the little bulb at the entrance of the neighbour's house, which is opposite my bedroom window. I hold my teddy bear in my arms. However, my body is trembling uncontrollably. My backache comes again. I haven't even noticed my tears flowing quietly. Another nightmare. This is my life.

Since my seventh birthday, I haven't celebrated anymore. I don't have any reason to celebrate in the future either, even if Vinny always says he'd like to do something for me. But anyway, he's not Joshua, the person who shared the same womb with me when our mother was pregnant.

I can hardly believe it.

I used to regard that horrible birthday twelve years ago as my entire lifelong scar. My parents got killed and Joshua got badly injured because he chose to protect me. Several operations saved his life even though he still had the fracture scar on his right leg. However, he fell accidently from the top floor of a hospital three years ago. God took him from my life forever. My whole family. Now I have almost no one to share my real emotions with. People always judge, comment and express their sympathy, but they can never really wear other's shoes, even relatives. I don't believe there is anyone else who understands me. No matter what success I achieve during my life, there is always somewhere empty in my heart. Sometimes I really want to have a cup of tea, or hot chocolate, or coffee, whatever it is, with my whole family, to get rid of the bad energy from my workplace, my current life. I don't get the point of people saying, "They're here, but you can't see them." What does that mean to me? I want to hug them, not just imagine them.

"Are you okay, love? I heard you shouting a few minutes ago. Can I come in?" Ava's voice suddenly appears outside my bedroom.

"Yes, of course," I answer her and sit up in my bed, "I'm sorry I woke you up."

"No, I went to the toilet by chance and I heard you. Why apologise? I'm just worried about you."

She walks in and quietly sits beside me. I can see the sincerity in her blue eyes, and they are very warm as usual.

"Tell me."

These two simple words are like a trigger that make me burst into tears. If I hadn't opened the bedroom door on that day, the murderer wouldn't have seen Joshua. And he might be still here with me now. But I don't want to say this to her. Because once I start talking, I might never stop.

"Come here, love. It was never your fault, from the beginning until the end." She holds me tightly in her arms and rubs my hair.

I am almost lying on her shoulder. She doesn't say anything else to me but holds me for a very long time until I stop sobbing. I like it. It makes me feel much better. I don't have a sister, but I still have her as my cousin, my friend. And I have my lovely Auntie Emily and Uncle Ethan. And I have Vinny. I shouldn't have been feeling negative. I am not alone.

I fall asleep again until the next morning at 9 a.m. It is Saturday. Thank God, I don't need to work again today.

There are several messages on my Instagram and WhatsApp. Most of them are from Vinny and Ava. I smile and reply with a few funny emojis.

And then I notice another WhatsApp message.

Unknown number. No picture.

My breath seems to pause for a few seconds after I see the message.

YOUR BROTHER'S DEATH MAY NOT BE AN ACCIDENT. ONLY I KNOW THE TRUTH, JOEY.

3

"Is this the strange message you received this morning?" Vincent stares at Joey's phone screen. He scratches his head at a loss.

Joey is not looking at him and both fall silent for a few minutes.

"You know what..." Joey turns her face to him finally. "I always thought it was suspicious. I just didn't tell you. I never worked out why Joshua went to the hospital. And why the top floor. Also, he's not as careless as me. And he never mentioned anything about having a friend there or whatever. But if it wasn't an accident, what happened? Did someone kill him? If that's the truth, the murderer is the only person to know the truth, right? So, this person messaging me—"

"One second." Vincent lifts his hand and interrupts, "Why haven't you replied to him?"

"What should I say? He killed my brother! I'm wondering whether or not to call the police."

"Don't be silly, Joey." He sighs. "What are you going to say? Tell the police that an unknown number said something strange about Joshua's death? They'd say it's just a joke. Also, look, I don't think the murderer is stupid enough to do this. What would be the point? Maybe this guy was a witness, but he didn't say anything at the time because he was scared, and he's decided to tell you now. That makes more sense. So, if I were you, I'd reply and ask him what he knows and who he is. Do that."

Joey does not reply. She reopens her phone and starts typing.

Who are you? How did u know my brother? Joey is someone who can type with just one thumb.

Who I am is not important now.

She freezes. It only takes about five seconds for a response to come back. Ding ding. Another one.

I can tell you what I saw at that moment. There is something you should know.

Listen, she types back, I hope u are serious. Go ahead please.

Ding ding.

I can't tell you now I'm afraid. Let's meet tonight at 6 p.m. in front of Black Sheep Coffee. I will wear a blue jacket and a pair of blue jeans. Come alone.

Joey pauses and glances at Vincent.

Are you still there?

Yes I am. Why can't you tell me now?

Her message is quickly followed by a reply.

Because I want to let you know that I am not joking, and you can trust me. And remember, if I don't appear at 6, call the police immediately.

"What the hell?" She says the words and then types them.

But this time no reply comes back.

Vincent grabs her phone and calls the number. But no one answers. No more new messages.

"Shit."

"Do you think I need to go, Vinny?" Joey keeps her eyes on the phone screen, and finally she gives up waiting for new messages.

"I'm just thinking... why did he ask you to call the police? If he's feeling unsafe, why didn't he go to the police straight away?"

"Maybe he has already tried that, but it didn't work... I guess you're right, Vinny. He could be a witness. But I just... It's all so sudden, and I'm scared. I feel something bad may happen. But I still want to go. It's all about Joshua. I even dreamt about him yesterday..." She bites her lip and tries her best to stop the tears from coming.

"Don't worry, Joey. I'll go with you. Right behind you," he says firmly, glancing at his watch on his arm.

Less than two hours before 6 p.m.

4

Olivia Stretford sits in front of her office desk with her Teams meeting open on her laptop. After a few minutes, she clicks the cursor on the red "hang up" button. She shuts down her laptop immediately and tidies up her desk.

"Liv, thank you so much for your help on my training today. I will see you tomorrow."

"You're most welcome. Take care of yourself, okay? I'm always willing to help you."

Her smile vanishes immediately after her colleague turns his back to her. She sighs, grabs her bag and puts her laptop in, quickly searching for something inside: a little pocket containing a burner phone. No one else except her man knows she has two phones and two completely different faces. Now it was time to transfer.

She counts the number of written notes in the pocket and takes out one of them. The words on the note are written in blood.

YOU WILL PAY THE PRICE SOONER OR LATER.

She shivers, but quickly speaks to herself and checks her watch. "It's fine, Liv, it'll be okay."

A few minutes later, she is in her car. She reclines her seat, closes her eyes and picks up her burner phone. After the call, she leaves her car.

The street is very busy with a lot of people like her also finishing their work and getting ready for a drink, a date or even a party.

But she still attracts other's attention due to her swollen face when she steps into a small shop.

"Oh my God, are you all right, love?" a shop assistant asks her with concern.

"Thank you for asking, but don't worry. It's just because of my carelessness," she answers and gives a smile.

She finally leaves the shop with a cup of coffee, a prawn sandwich and some apples.

At the corner of the street, no one notices there is a man with earphones in both of his ears. He is wearing a black face mask and a pair of old Doc Martens, and his dark blue eyes never leave Olivia.

5

Joey

It is half past five in the evening. Only half an hour before the time the unknown messenger suggested.

I am on my way to the cafe. It is not very far away from my place, no more than a fifteen-minute walk. I try my best to stay calm, but it is a bit hard for me.

I don't know why I'm feeling like this. The unknown person did not sound aggressive, but he scares me. Does he think his life will be in danger and that's why he asked me to call the police if he didn't come? And if that's true, maybe it's better for him to keep silent. But he must know something, because everyone thinks Joshua's death was an accident, even the police. And there were no witnesses three years ago. So, when he said it was not an accident, I could hardly force myself to ignore his message.

I turn around and try to see Vinny. He is not walking straight behind me. Instead, he is at the opposite end of the road with his mobile phone close to his ear.

I am not in a relationship with Vinny, but I always feel much better and a sense of safety when he is with me. There are always people who tell us we should be lovers, but I have no idea whether I'm ready for a relationship. He has also never expressed those kinds of ideas to me. I still prefer our current situation.

Suddenly, Vinny's message comes.

DON'T LOOK AT ME, JOEY, JUST IN CASE. I WILL NEVER LEAVE YOU ALONE, DON'T WORRY, TRUST ME.

Almost there. I am approaching Black Sheep Coffee, but I don't see a person in blue around.

It is 5:54 p.m.

I hesitate for a moment, but finally walk into the cafe. I ask for a mocha latte, and choose a seat by the window, which allows me to keep an eye on the opposite road and the pedestrians coming from both sides of the cafe. There is a crossroad, so there are still loads of people, buses and vehicles around. I need to pay full attention. I can feel my heart beating quickly, and I find it hard to keep sitting calmly. Still, nobody approaches me. There are a few people around me who are wearing blue, but they are either one of a couple, or the ones who concentrate on their newspapers and books. No eye contact. No messages from that unknown number.

ARE YOU AROUND? I AM WAITING FOR YOU HERE.

No response. No "online" status. No call back.

6

Laura Williams' office area is occupied with a computer, a phone, a fax and piles of files and papers. She frowns at the screen of her laptop and types quickly. This is not something she likes. She has loads of reports to complete. The who, when, how, where and what. There was a larceny a few days ago, so she has to get the exact items taken, their values, the contact details of the owner, any witnesses, etc. Life was not easy for people like her.

And then she sees two young people coming towards the police station. The girl is grabbing her mobile phone and seems like she wants to show it to someone at once. Her long chestnut hair is a bit messy, which matches her sporty look. A Caucasian young man is walking alongside her. He is average-looking, but his dazzling golden hair and his tall build make him look charming. Both seem under twenty-five years old.

"Good morning, are you guys all right? How can I help?" Laura greets them.

"Umm... Hello. I got a strange message from an unknown number. But I don't think it was a prank."

Joey's voice sounds hesitating, but she passes her mobile phone to Laura almost at the same time.

"Her brother died in an accident three years ago, but it seems like this person is trying to tell us the truth and asked us to meet him. But he didn't appear." Vincent stares at Laura.

"That's strange. May I ask for your name and basic information please? Is that okay?"

"Yes, my name is Joey Palmer. And he is my friend, Vincent King."

Laura smiles and types a few words in the computer as she asks them a few basic questions. "So, Miss Palmer, may I have that unknown number who texted you?"

"Yes. Call me Joey please."

"Cool. So, Joey, we'll try to track this number if we can. But the user might have turned off the phone or changed the settings to make it untraceable. If we have news, we'll be in touch…"

"One second… is that all you can do at this point?"

"Unfortunately, yes." Laura shrugs and gives them a helpless smile. "At this point, we can't do much. I'm so sorry. The WhatsApp messages can't be traced unless you ask for a court warrant, and that's usually for serious criminal cases. But nothing really happened, right? If I report this to my boss, she might say the same. She might even suggest it's just a prank. Of course, I know the situation might be different for you. My sister also passed away due to an accident. If I were you, I would feel the same about wanting the truth. I'll check whether there are any detectives available now and ask them to have a chat with you guys. But it may take a while, do you want to wait a bit?"

Vincent opens his mouth to say something, but Joey stops him. At first, she has the impression that all police officers are cold, serious and business-like. But this girl seems different. She's not judging, and she seems sincere and warm. Having a chat with a detective may be a good choice. Maybe a detective will have some resources to find more details about Joshua's fall from the top of the hospital, such as any potential witnesses. It could be helpful to dig in.

"Thank you so much. We'll wait for a while..."

Just after Joey finishes her sentence, a young man suddenly appears and interrupts the conversation.

"Laura, do you have the details of last week's robbery—My God, Vinny, why are you here?"

Joey stares at him. He looks like he's in his mid-twenties, with brown hair that extends to his earlobes.

His deep eyes are filled with surprise. He's wearing a blue leather jacket and a pair of leather boots. Although he's not as tall as Vincent, he looks a bit more capable.

"Chris? It's you!" Vincent looks confused, but he begins to feel excited after a few seconds and hugs his old friend. He used to be on the football team when he was an undergraduate at Edinburgh University, and this guy in front of him, Chris Bambos, was also one of the members, but he was studying for his master's at that time. They were very good friends, but they almost lost contact after Chris went to Oxford to start his PhD.

"Wow, I never expected you guys to already know each other," Laura says, "That's perfect. Detective Bambos just joined us two months ago. By the way, why are you here, Chris? You should be on leave."

"My dad wasn't feeling very well yesterday," Chris says, "We had to cancel our family trip to the Highlands. I just told the boss I'm back, then I came here and found my bro. I'm happy that the trip was cancelled." He smiles, and then his attention turns to Joey. "Is she your girlfriend, Vinny?"

"Shut up." Vincent laughs and looks at Joey. He wishes it was true. "This is Joey, my friend, and she received some strange messages yesterday. That's why we came here to ask for help from the police."

Chris offers his hand to Joey.

"Yes, I just recorded their basic information and the general case," Laura says, showing what she just recorded to Chris. "But it would be helpful for you to have a chat with your old friend about the details seriously. Is that okay with you? Or do you have something more urgent to do?"

"Nope. Of course I'm happy to," Chris says in a calm voice. "Right, guys, do you mind following me to that small room and we can talk?"

They enter a small meeting room.

"Is tea okay for both of you?"

"That would be great," Joey says.

"Okay. So, what kind of messages did you receive, Joey? Is this a stalker?" Chris offers them two cups of English breakfast tea.

"No. To be honest, my brother passed away due to an accident three years ago. He fell from the top floor of a hospital. This was regarded as an accident. And yesterday an unknown number texted me, and he said he knew the truth about the accident and asked me to meet him. But he never appeared, and he asked me to call the police if he didn't show up."

"One second... I think I remember the accident.

I was still in Edinburgh at that time before I went to Oxford to start my PhD. The news reported it, and I remember it happened at the John Radcliffe Hospital, is that right?"

"Yes, that's it." Joey's eyes glow. "But there were no witnesses at that time. It was suspicious but not much evidence…"

Suddenly Chris' mobile phone rings.

"Sorry," Chris says, picking up his phone, "Hello, Detective Bambos speaking."

Both Joey and Vincent notice Chris' expression turning serious immediately after he hears something on the phone.

"Sure. I see. I'll be there in half an hour… I'm terribly sorry," he apologises sincerely, handing his calling cards to his two friends, "But I need to go. It's sudden. Here's my number. Call me back tomorrow and I'll be available. I promise."

Then he leaves the police station in a hurry.

7

Chris zigzags through the crowd around the detached house in Northampton Road and approaches the cordon. An officer greets him over there and passes him to another man.

"Detective Bambos?" he asks with his emotionless eyes staring at Chris. His solid form towers over Chris and the other officers.

Chris nods.

"I'm Detective Dawson. We had the call this morning." The man shakes hands with Chris and continues. "The resident of this house called the police. She said she accidently killed a man who had been stalking and scaring her for a long time. This morning she was attacked by the victim. When we arrived, she was also badly injured and sent to the nearby hospital. But, of course, I'll give you the address of the hospital and you can interview her for further investigation."

"Are the forensic team on their way? Any witnesses?" Chris asks, looking around without noticing any forensic stuff.

"No, as I mentioned on the phone, I usually focus on theft and burglaries, and I was called here by mistake,"

Dawson says, "You're always in charge of violent crimes like this. I think this case might be a bit complex as you might have to spend some time figuring out the identity and the past activities of this victim. You need to judge whether it was self-defence. Everything stayed untouched. The officer over there will provide you with gloves and shoe covers."

Chris gives him a thumb-up gesture and then has a quick call to the forensic team and his partner.

"What I know is that the resident is called Olivia Stretford, thirty-five years old, and she lives on her own in this house. She used to live with a roommate, but her roommate relocated to Reading one year ago. Now she's staying here in a two-bedroom house. But, of course, this house is for rent, so she needs to pay for the whole house. Look, I need to go now as I have another case about domestic abuse in my department, and I need to work on that. Good luck, mate." His tone turns into a happier one and he even blinks.

"No problem. Thank you for your help here."

Chris faces the house after Dawson drives away. "That's almost the same time," he says to himself. Just one hour ago, his old friend was calling the police for something strange. It was such a big coincidence. Or, they had connections.

The house is a small one-storey detached house with a grey tiled roof. The main door does not face the main road; instead, Chris has to walk towards the right edge of the wall where there is a white-framed door. No garage, but there is a big space with so many little stones in front of the house. More than enough space to fit two cars.

"Chris!"

When Chris is about to open the door handle, a man gets out of his car and greets him. He is sweating, with a bottle of Pepsi in his hand.

"Here you are, Jordan. Let's have a look."

Jordan pulls off his sunglasses and nods.

Once they step into the house, a strong bloody smell bursts into their noses. The blood extends from the kitchen to the living room, which is attached to the kitchen. The lifeless body is lying in a corner of the dining area with a knife slanted into his chest. The man looks to be in in his fifties, of medium height, with dark curly hair. He is wearing a tattered long-sleeved shirt and a pair of jeans. His arms are spread, and his eyes are open, staring straight at the ceiling. His face looks terrifying and ferocious. It's clear he must have been filled with hatred before his death.

The two young detectives stay silent for a while. They have seen a few murder scenes before, but the expression on this victim makes them shudder. From his eyes, they do not see fear. Instead, there is anger, violence, sadness and evil.

"I don't think I can look at his eyes anymore," Jordan says, turning his back to the body and covering his eyes with his hands.

Chris is standing still and staring at the body. It seems like the only fatal wound is on the left side of the man's chest. However, his face has a few scratches, which were likely caused by the woman's nails. Chris' gaze finally leaves the body and he begins to look around the surroundings.

The dining area and the small living room are just between the two bedrooms. It's not hard to identify the one that belongs to Olivia. Her bedroom door is not fully closed, with a jacket hanging over it. Her bedroom also has a locked French window which faces the back garden. The garden is enclosed by wooden fences. Outside the fences there are a few trees and another road. However, the fences are not taller than two metres, which means someone could climb over them and get into the back garden. But even though that was possible, a key would still be required to get to Olivia's bedroom.

Before the forensic team arrive, Chris and his partner try to find any signs of a break-in, but they don't find any.

"I remember you said the deceased was likely a stalker." Jordan crosses the body and looks at the main door, "But if that's true, how did he get into the room without breaking into the house?"

"In that case, there's one possibility, Jordan." Chris smiles. "The resident opened the door for the victim."

8

Joey

I went back home straight away after we meet Chris in the police station.

It's II a.m. the next day, and I'm already exhausted. I would like something to eat. Just then, I smell something nice.

Auntie Emily is cooking in the kitchen. She doesn't notice me behind her and I hug her from the back.

"I know that's you, sweetheart." She laughs, turns around and kisses me on my cheek, "Your uncle went to the gym as usual early this morning. Ava still hasn't come out from her room, and I guess that lazy cat is still sleeping. You guys all left me alone this sunny Sunday." She pretends to be annoyed, but her raised lips betray her.

I don't move but still hug her. She is wearing a pink apron with a soft sweater. I see there is some toast, scrambled eggs and grilled tomatoes.

Suddenly my memory is back to the days before I was seven. I was always around my mum when she was cooking. One reason was that I enjoyed seeing when the food was going to be ready; another reason was that my mum was still a good storyteller even when she was cooking. Her voice was always gentle, soft and comforting. Every time I was clingy when she was cooking, Joshua would say, "Joey, come with me, don't let Mummy get exhausted." Although he was only ten minutes older than me, his behaviour was more mature, just like he was five years older than me.

I don't notice my tears falling until my aunt touches my hands which are around her waist.

"The food is ready. Have some breakfast with me, okay, honey?" Aunt Emily says, trying to remove my hands and pick up the dishes. "My God, you all right?"

She makes me face her and wipes away my tears by hands. "Who made my girl cry? I will cut his fingers."

"I'm all right. I just... I just feel that it's so lovely to stay with you and..." I sob and try to finish the answer, but I fail.

"My silly girl," she says, hugging me again. For a very long time this time.

I close my eyes. I used to think that I was calm enough for everything, until I saw that message. It broke into the deepest part of my heart. It crashed into my new life. I couldn't ignore it. Now, was there anything

I could do to find the truth by myself? Or with Chris' help? Should I tell Auntie and Uncle? Or at least Ava?

Just then, the door of Ava's bedroom opens. "Good morning, Mum! Wow, you're getting intimate this morning."

I quickly wipe my tears and come out from Emily's arms. "Shut up. I'm not like you." I laugh. "Tired? How was your sleep?"

"Amazing." Ava blows me a kiss. "Now I'm happy. I'm hungry, Mum."

At the same time, Aunt Emily has prepared English breakfast tea with some milk in it. As we are going to eat, the door opens and Uncle Ethan is carrying a watermelon in his arms, and he almost drops it.

"Dad, be careful." Ava smiles. "Good morning."

"Morning. You're all here. That's not usual. Nice weather, isn't it? I even sweated." He gives Auntie a kiss and then faces us. "You should have told me you got food ready. I wouldn't have had toast outside."

"That's not my fault. You never let me know you're hungry."

I have some scrambled eggs and share some funny work stories with them. After that, I go back to my own room.

It is always nice when I hang out with them. I feel relaxed and comforted. No, I don't want them to know about the messages. At least not now. I like their smiling faces. I'm not going to destroy the precious happiness. I will let them know when the time is perfect.

Suddenly the doorbell rings and I hear Auntie Emily's voice.

"Hi, who are you guys looking for? Vinny! Are you looking for Joey?"

"Hello, good morning, how are you? Yes, we're here to play escape room games with Joey. We can't wait! This is Chris, my bro."

"Hello, hope I'm not bothering you."

I come out of my room and stare at Chris. He has changed into another style. He is wearing a big white jumper with a pair of joggers, which makes him look much younger. Aunt Emily seems quite excited. She asks my uncle to wash the dishes, and she leaves us three after she says, "Make yourselves at home."

We exchange eye contact with each other and Vinny and Chris come to my room and close the door without any hesitation.

"I just left the forensic team to do further investigations," Chris says, "They will contact me with any more details. But what I know is that the doctor assumes the time of death was between midnight and yesterday morning."

"The time was quite close." I look at him, even though I have no idea whether I'm asking him or drawing a conclusion by myself.

"We won't know that for sure. You know it usually takes time before a body is found out. Now we haven't got any murder cases or missing person reports, but we need to see what will happen in the next few days. Luckily, the identities of both the victim and the lady who claimed she accidently killed him were both confirmed. I'm here to visit you because both of them were born in Edinburgh." Chris passes me two photos. "Have you seen these two before?"

I carefully check the photos and search for my memory bit by bit. One of them is an old man, who looks between the age of fifty-five and sixty-five. The other photo is a charming middle-aged woman with straight brown hair. However, nothing comes to mind. I shake my head with helplessness.

"Who is the victim?" Vinny suddenly asks.

"The old man is Peter Wilson. Unemployed. He used to have a son, but he passed away many years ago.

He has a nephew, but not in Oxford. And this lady is called Olivia Stretford, thirty-five years old. From what I heard from other officers, it seemed like he had been stalking her for a while."

"He's a stalker? But he was killed. What the hell?" Vinny looks confused.

"That's why I told you it's unclear just now," Chris says, "We need to do more examinations at the scene to check for fingerprints and any CCTV footage. And also, Olivia might have acted in self-defence, because she was the one who called the police. She was also badly injured and sent to hospital. I am going to interview her tomorrow for more details."

"I see." Vinny lowers his head.

"That means it's hard to decide who sent me the messages, if there are connections between these." I sigh.

"Exactly. Most people may think Olivia might be the one, because she got stalked, even attacked, by the stalker, and she called the police herself," Chris says becoming serious, "But there is another possibility. It's not very likely, but it might be the case."

"What's that?"

"She is the actual murderer."

9

Once they get back to the police station, Chris and Jordan decide to split their investigation. Jordan would visit Peter Wilson's nephew to know more about his personal life, while Chris was willing to go to the hospital to have a chat with Olivia Stretford. This morning he had already made a call to the hospital to ask the doctor about Olivia's injuries and whether it was possible for him to have a quick visit.

His instinct tells him that this case may have connections to Joey's brother somehow, but he has no evidence yet. After he visited Joey this morning, he tried to dig into Olivia's background. However, nothing looked dodgy, especially in the last three years. Olivia was just a decent woman working as a scientist in an industrial lab at present. She had been working in the same workplace for four years. Single. No kids. Although she was born in Edinburgh, her family moved to Oxford when she was in junior high school. Some information showed that her parents relocated to Oxford because of their new jobs.

It only takes Chris around eight minutes to drive to the hospital. He greets the nurse on the counter and then he walks to Olivia's room: 301, the closest room to the stairs. He knocks gently three times, then he hears a few footsteps approaching the door.

"Hello, are you Detective Bambos? Please come in." A doctor smiles at him. "We spoke on the phone. As I said, her head was hit by a blunt object, and there is a knife wound on her lower back. I can't say it's serious, but she was somewhat frightened by the incident. So, please don't take too long."

The doctor gives Olivia a sympathetic look and leaves the room.

Chris nods and has a quick look at Olivia. She has a bandage tied around her head. Her face is a bit swollen, which makes it clear that she got hit there. Her pale face shows she is very weak now. She looks at Chris, and a smile squeezes out of her dry lips.

"Miss Stretford..." Chris chooses his words carefully, trying not to be too serious as a usual cop. "I'm Detective Bambos. I'm really sorry about what you experienced. How are you feeling now?"

Olivia moves her lips, but she is soundless. She clears her throat and gazes at Chris before she finally begins to speak.

"Thank you, detective." Her voice is hoarse. "At least I'm alive. I'm sorry... I didn't mean to kill that person, but he-he pretended to be a delivery man in the morning and attacked me in my house. I-I..." She bursts into tears.

Chris offers her a few tissues, which she accepts. She covers her eyes and sobs.

"Why? I just didn't know when it would end. He was stalking me everywhere, sending me scary messages, leaving me notes."

Chris doesn't answer her or ask follow-up questions. He knows she was not actually asking him; instead, she was just letting out her fear, stress and hatred. He knows he should give her time and wait for her to continue.

"I had this kind of life for almost two years. I never got a wink of sleep. He knew my number. He knew where I lived. He knew my workplace. He knew everything. Sometimes he knocked on my front door in the evenings. Luckily, my front door is the type that you can see who's outside. Then I would receive his note in the morning or his messages. I knew it was him. But he never appeared. Never let me see his face. Never really attacked me."

Chris is about to speak, but she continues before he opens his mouth.

"But... as he was always there, I never assumed he was ready to attack me, to make me feel pain." She begins to cry instead of sob. "Now I've killed him. Tell me, detective, what should I do? Are you here to arrest me?"

Chris walks closer to her bed and takes a seat. "No, Miss Stretford. I'm not here because of that. As a detective, it's always my responsibility to figure out what exactly happened. I need more details, and then I can help you. Look, I can see it might have been self-defence. But I need some more details to prove that. So, your words are always the most important for me to investigate."

Olivia calms down a bit and tries to sit up. With his concerned eyes, she finally replies.

"Okay. I can tell you everything, detective. By the way, please call me Olivia."

"Thank you, Olivia. I really appreciate that," Chris says, "To begin with, you mentioned that he was stalking you for a long time. Did you know this person before?"

Chris notices her pupils dilate for one second then look down, but back to normal at once. Her hands grasp the duvet.

"No. Not at all." She shakes her head. "I don't know why he was stalking me."

"Okay," Chris answers, giving her a comforting smile, "But I'm a bit confused here, Olivia. I guess you must have felt scared, so why you didn't call the police, not even once?"

Olivia looks down again. She is trying to touch her neck, then her tears come again.

"Sorry, Olivia. I apologise for making you feel uncomfortable. I know this is hard for you."

"That's all right, detective. I'm just a bit... traumatised. I just didn't think the police could do much about it. And at first, I thought it was just a prank, or someone hated me and wanted me to feel scared, but not serious, like what happened yesterday morning."

"I see. I would like to know more about the details of what happened yesterday morning. You said he pretended to be a delivery man. Do you remember what time that was?"

"Umm... let me see. I think it was just after eight. Maybe five past eight or something. Because my shift starts at nine, so I leave home at around eight. I was about to leave but I couldn't find my keys. So, I walked into the living room to look for them. And then he was knocking at my door."

"Okay, that makes sense. So, you just opened the door then?"

"Yes, because I was in a hurry," Olivia answers, lowering her voice. "And I just wanted to find my keys and go to work. Also, I could see through the door that the person on the other side was standing there with a big box. And I did buy a big bookshelf a few days ago. Then I opened the door..."

"And then he attacked you?" Chris follows her words and adds a summary. To his surprise, Olivia does not nod at once.

"Yes," she finally says.

"Okay. Thank you, Olivia." Chris makes some notes quickly and continues. "Now listen. I need your help with our investigation. Stalkers usually stalk someone with a reason. Of course, we don't know this right now, but we're going to find any possible connection between him and you..."

"But I told you I didn't know him, detective." There is a confused look on her face.

"Yes, I know," Chris replies, "Don't worry. What I need you to do is to dig in your memory a bit. What we noticed was this guy, Peter Wilson, was a local in Edinburgh. Have you been to Edinburgh before?"

"Yes. Actually, I was born there. But I left there because of the relocation of my parents," she answers.

Chris stares at her with a suspicious look.

"It doesn't mean anything, detective." Her voice suddenly becomes cold. "You can't say we had a connection before because of the same place we come from. It's ridiculous."

"Of course." Chris ignores her unpleased tone and continues. "But have you thought about this possibility: he knows you, but you don't? You left Edinburgh when you were in junior high school. Think about that. Nothing happened during that time?"

"Please don't talk nonsense, detective. I was just a teenager. What do you think I did back then to make an old guy stalk me after several years?"

"One second." Chris stares at her suddenly. "I never talked about his age, Olivia. From his photo, I can't guess his age as he looks strong, and he's also dyed his hair. But he is in his sixties. How could you describe him as 'old'? I don't think you'd have enough time to judge that during the seconds of being attacked?"

"It was just a first impression," she answers firmly.

"Okay. That makes sense," he finally says with a gentle tone, not wanting to push further today, "I hope you recover soon, Olivia. If you remember something or you need anything, no matter how tiny it is, call me any time. Thank you very much for your time today." He passes his card to her.

She accepts his card and nods.

He turns around and is about to leave, so he doesn't see the misery in her eyes.

"Detective…" she suddenly calls out in a weak voice before he leaves the room, "I kept the notes."

He faces her, waiting for her following words.

"The notes from him which he tried to scare me with. I kept them all. My bag. It's in my room."

10

Joey

I can't sleep after the call with Chris.

I don't know who Olivia is. I never met her. But Chris says she must have known Peter before, but she is hiding this fact.

Perhaps she was the one who texted me as an unknown number, and that's why she doesn't want others to know that. And she got attacked by that guy called Peter. If that's true, then Peter might be the one related to my brother's death.

No. It can't be so straightforward because Peter is dead now. No more threat. If I was Olivia, I would tell the police everything rather than keeping it to myself, unless there is someone else involved in my brother's case. And we don't know this person yet.

If Peter is the one who texted me, then Olivia is not only a murderer who pretended to be attacked, but also someone related to my brother's death. But Chris told me they found notes in Olivia's bag, and they are confirmed to be in Peter Wilson's handwriting. It's not likely that Olivia is trying to pretend she had a stalker and mimic his handwriting. That would be crazy.

Or was it someone else who texted me? Maybe this case isn't even associated with the unknown number? Everything is just due to my overthinking.

There must be something else. Come on. I have to do something.

I open my phone and reread the messages from the unknown number.

Your brother's death may not be an accident.

Wait one second...

***

One year before Joey's parents' death

The weather was suddenly turning windy. It was even worse when it was close to the sea.

"Come on, kids. We need to leave now," their mother said, pointing at their black car nearby. She looked a bit exhausted and faced her husband.

"Do we need to go home now?" Joey asked. She looked disappointed and stopped moving. "I still haven't had enough. What secrets do you have, Mum?"

She saw her mum and dad whispering to each other.

"It's not a secret, love. We're going to tell both of you a story later. It happened before you were born."

Joshua was also attracted by her words. This time they became quiet, opening the car door and sitting down.

The car stopped after about fifteen minutes.

There were hundreds of gravestones with flowers beside them. Joshua and Joey followed their parents to a monument.

MASON PALMER

BELOVED SON OF OLIVER AND SARAH

(24 JUNE 1988–09 OCTOBER 2000)

REST IN PEACE, OUR ANGEL

Joey noticed her mum wiping tears on her cheek without saying a word.

"You had a big brother before you were born," their father said with a peaceful voice, "But we didn't protect him well."

"Where is he now?" Joey asked. At her age, she did not have a clear understanding of death.

Joshua stayed quiet. His eyes stared at the words on the monument.

"He's here, love." Her father knelt down and faced them. "You can't see him. He turned into air, the flowers, the grass. He's everywhere. He used to be the same as you two, but we made some mistakes, and he decided to change into another form of existence."

"That sounds magic," said Joey, "Dad, is this magic? But it's sad that I can't see my big brother."

"Yes, it's a shame. That's why your mum is sad. Just after your big brother left, we had you two. You two were gifts from God after we went through this. Bur remember my words, Joey." He held both of them in his arms. "We were punished because we failed to take care of him. He also didn't take care of himself. Promise me, you two, we love you very much. Please take care of yourselves."

"I see, Dad. I don't want Mum to be sad again," Joshua answered.

Joey moved away her dad's hand and hugged her mum from behind.

"I'm sorry, Mum. I shouldn't have run everywhere this afternoon. I'll take care of myself. I won't make you sad," she murmured, then faced the monument. "Mason, nice to meet you. My name's Joey. I'm your younger sister. You have another brother called Joshua. We're all good. We love you."

Her mother was shivering with tears after she said these words. As a child, Joey could not understand death. But she was sensitive enough to feel the emotion.

***

Yes, I had a big brother who was born before Joshua and me. Just a few days ago, I remembered this memory when Auntie Emily mentioned how busy my parents were when they got their first kid.

But the unknown messages only mentioned "my brother". It doesn't mention Joshua's name. But I actually have two. Is it possible they weren't referring to Joshua? Maybe it refers to my big brother, Mason, who passed away before my parents. If so, how could it be linked to me? I almost know nothing about what happened to him. My brain is now filled with a mess about the weird messages, about Olivia's words, about my two brothers, even about my parents. My life has always been full of a lot of mysteries, and they are never solved.

My parents only mentioned Mason once on that day. To be honest, I even forgot about him after all these years, which suddenly makes me feel guilty. On that day, I was too young to understand what death was. If my parents were still here with me, I might know more about my big brother. After my parents' death, almost no one remembered him again. If the unknown messages hadn't crashed into my life, I would never have remembered either. If he was still alive now, he would be thirty-five years old.

That would be the same age as Olivia.

I suddenly freeze.

I sit at my desk and open my laptop. Could it be possible that something else happened several years ago except for my parents' death? Now I'm not pretty sure of that, but there are too many coincidences. Olivia and Mason are the same age, and they are all local from Edinburgh, so they might have studied at the same junior high school at the age of twelve. The age Mason lost his life. Edinburgh isn't that big. I have no idea about Peter, but if there's any link between Olivia and Mason and what happened to Mason, then probably the mystery will be figured out a bit. Google is the only tool for me to search out something now, even though I don't expect much from it.

I open Chrome and type "Olivia Stretford" in the search box. Wow, 5,350,000 results. It doesn't surprise me. Olivia is a common name. The first page is filled with lots of pictures of people who are called Olivia Stretford. I scroll down a bit, and then it comes to some Twitter and LinkedIn accounts. No information related to the Olivia I'm looking for. No good. I need to narrow the results. I try a few specific combinations such as "Olivia Stretford Edinburgh" or "Olivia Stretford Oxford". The latter result produces some hits: a LinkedIn profile, a few Instagram accounts, and a Facebook page.

I click on the link of the LinkedIn profile. Here it is. I recognise the headshot immediately. A full professional photo of Olivia in a dark blue suit, looking stunning and confident in the camera. However, there's not too much information on the profile.

> SEP 2006 TO JUNE 2009. BSc UNIVERSITY OF
> OXFORD, MEDICINAL SCIENCE
> JULY 2009 TO OCT 2013. PhD UNIVERSITY OF
> OXFORD

That's it. No more previous information. That makes sense because no one would add information before university. I have no interest in her career, because it would have happened before she went to university, and before Oxford. Unfortunately, there's almost no information about her in Edinburgh.

It's too early to give up now. I can't find anything about Olivia, but maybe I can find something else, like the news in 2000. The year my big brother passed away.

I type another search "2000 Edinburgh news". The first page looks very general. The results come out with "fifteen photos that capture Edinburgh in 2000" and other irrelevant information such as the nightclubs in Edinburgh. I laugh to myself. If I can easily find all this, then why do we need police?

But I keep scrolling down and turn to page two, page three. Anything, please. There's nothing special until I am attracted by a link from the Herald Scotland website on page five.

STUDENT PUNCH-UP IN JUNIOR HIGH SCHOOL. TWO VICTIMS.

09 OCTOBER 2000

TWO TWELVE-YEAR-OLD TEENAGERS DIED DURING A PUNCH-UP AT GEORGE WOOD HIGH SCHOOL. THE STUDENTS WERE BEING VIOLENTLY BULLIED, ACCORDING TO TEACHERS FROM THE SCHOOL. A FEW OF THE OTHER PUPILS WERE ALSO INVOLVED.

WITNESSES SAY THE INCIDENT HAPPENED JUST AFTER SCHOOL.

THE TWO STUDENTS WERE SENT TO THE NEARBY
HOSPITAL BUT DIED A SHORT TIME LATER.

ADAM WILSON, THE COUSIN OF ONE OF THE
VICTIMS, POSTED ON FACEBOOK: "I AM ABSOLUTELY
TRAUMATISED BY WHAT HAPPENED TO MY COUSIN. HE
WAS ALWAYS KIND, HELPFUL AND BRILLIANT. I WILL
NEVER FORGIVE THE ONES WHO BULLIED HIM."

POLICE SCOTLAND CLAIM THEY ARE STILL
INVESTIGATING MORE DETAILS.

I'm attracted to the story because George Wood High
School is just a few minutes away from my original
place in Edinburgh, with my parents and Joshua.
My parents worked in Chalmers Centre, a hospital,
and they did mention that they saw a lot of students
around the area. I even remember previously there was
a discussion between my parents about which school
they would like to send us to. However, I can't remember
how many schools got included in the discussion, but
I did feel surprised that they finally didn't send us to
George Wood High School as it was both close to our
home and their hospital.

And then I saw this piece of news.

A strong instinct tells me it is related to what is going on at the moment, but I have no evidence. I don't know any names of the victims and no other further details. I need more help.

Then suddenly something comes to my mind. When Chris was showing me the photo of the male victim, I remember there was a note at the edge of the photo which noted his name.

Peter Wilson.

Adam Wilson.

I take a screenshot of the article and send it to Chris.

II

"Good morning." Jordan is carrying his backpack, staggering the last few steps into the office with a cup of coffee in his hand.

"Morning." Chris stares at his laptop, then glances at him. "Are you all right? You look exhausted."

"I'm fine. Just running late," Jordan replies and puts down his backpack, "By the way, I visited Peter Wilson's nephew and he told me something about Peter's personal life. Well, he is a tough guy, to be honest, and he told me his uncle never talked about someone called Olivia. Nothing out of the ordinary except for one thing."

Chris doesn't answer, waiting for Jordan's words.

"Peter Wilson used to have a son, but the boy died due to school bullying several years ago."

Chris takes a deep breath. "Good job. I only have one question to ask you."

"Yes?"

"Tell me the name of his nephew."

"Adam Wilson," Jordan answers, "Anything wrong?"

"Hold on. I'll explain to you in a second." Chris types quickly on his laptop. Just then, the boss, Chief

Inspector Dale, steps into the office without knocking at the door.

"Morning, ma'am," Chris greets her simply.

"I might need you to explain this to me, Chris." She walks around Chris' seat and sits on the sofa, "Laura has told me what has happened these last few days. I fully understand that you would like to scratch any likely clues, Chris. I always appreciate that. But the thing is, it's almost confirmed that the lady was acting in self-defence. We've explored her room and found a few warning notes from the victim. It was confirmed by his nephew that they were in his handwriting. The forensic team also mentioned the victim only had one fatal wound, and fingerprints were found on the knife. So, I wonder why you want to link this to a girl who received some weird messages from an unknown number. We get so many of these cases, and most of them are proved to be a prank."

"Yes, you're right, ma'am." Chris slightly nods, "I also thought that at first, but there are a few points I'm suspicious about."

"Go on," she replies, grabbing a cup of coffee and looking at Chris.

"I had a small chat with Olivia in the hospital, and I think she is definitely hiding something," he says firmly, "Both Olivia and Peter were locals in Edinburgh. When I asked her whether she knew Peter before, her reaction was a bit weird. One fact is, a stalker always has a reason, no matter how tiny it is. It is important for us to figure out why he was stalking her. Also, only having the matching handwriting does not a hundred percent support the hypothesis. In other words, I think she's lying. If that's true, this might not be self-defence. It might be murder."

"So, you think she actually knew the victim?"

"Yes, but of course it's only a hypothesis."

"Okay," Dale answers, "But even if that's true, why are you trying to link it to the messages? What's the possible connection? Or have you found out some more clues?

"Yes." Jordan raises his hand. "I spoke to Peter's nephew yesterday, and he told me Peter used to have a son, but he died several years ago. I just calculated the time and his son would be a similar age to Olivia."

"Actually, you're right." Chris smiles and continues, "The girl who received the messages talking about her brother, Joey Palmer, sent me this yesterday. She said she found it from this news article in 2000."

He passes his mobile phone to both of his colleagues.

"Oh my God, that's the name," says Jordan. "That's why you were asking me just now."

"Exactly. Peter's son was one of the two boys who died in the school bullying incident. He was called Tracy Wilson. And another boy... I tried to check this with the Scottish police this morning. They told me he was called Mason Palmer, and he was Joey's brother."

Jordan looks shocked.

"I see your point, Chris," Dale lowers her head and says, "But what about Olivia? Have you checked whether she was their classmate, or anything linked?"

"Unfortunately, not yet," Chris answers, "But there must be a link somewhere. I'm planning to check with the school where Mason and Tracy used to go, and perhaps see whether there was a student called Olivia Stretford, or any other related possibilities. I'm sure there should be something there."

"Then the story might be something like Olivia was bullying his son. I can't think about any other reasons." Jordan stands from his seat and faces Chris.

"I would be happy if it was that simple," Chris says, "We don't know what really happened on that day. The Scottish police told me this case was not investigated deeply. What they did was just question some of the witnesses. They just regarded it as an accident."

"Better to check it out," Dale replies. "Have we talked with anyone from Olivia's family? How much do you know about Olivia's background?"

"I had a call with her mother yesterday evening." Jordan takes out his notebook. "Her parents lived in Abingdon, quite close to Oxford. Olivia is not their only child. She has a sister who works in the US, so she's usually not in the UK. To be honest, I don't think Olivia is very close to her parents, even a bit indifferent. Her mother didn't even ask me how her daughter's injuries were. Anyway, Olivia is a decent woman. She graduated from Oxford and then started a job as a scientist immediately after graduation. We haven't talked to her colleagues, but she looks fine. No criminal records either."

Chris' mind suddenly bumps back to the conversation with Olivia in the hospital. She was alone there. Her pale face, her peeling lips. No one was with her except that considerate doctor.

"Hold on." Dale looks confused and faces Chris, "I remember you said she was born in Edinburgh, not Oxford."

"Yes, she told me she was local there," Chris answers. There is a silence for a few seconds.

"I still think she's probably just a poor lady who got stalked and tried to defend herself," Dale finally says. "She got stalked because she bullied others. The man broke into her house as he was going to get revenge, and she tried to protect herself. Think about it. If she had actually wanted to kill the man, why would she tell you she was from Edinburgh? This would make us dig into the link with the victim. She could just say she was local in Oxford and didn't know the man, that's it. No more explanation. You wouldn't have needed to ask her any more questions."

"That makes sense," Jordan says.

"Another point is," Dale continues, "If she wanted to kill someone, she'd need to make sure that this guy broke into her house for her to kill him. How could she know when a stalker would break into her house? She'd have to plan. Prepare. Right?"

"Peter didn't break into her house, ma'am," Chris tries to argue, "Olivia told me she opened the door for him. And we checked her house as well. No forced entry."

"What's the difference then?" she answers firmly, "It was still unpredictable. Please don't tell me you think this poor lady already knew exactly when the man would arrive. If that happened, they were cooperating with each other. But of course, that's impossible."

"I still haven't checked Peter Wilson's house yet, by the way, but I'll go today," Jordan adds.

"That would be great. Anyway, I don't think this is a complex case, guys," Dale says, "There are still a few points we need to check out, just in case. But I don't think there's a long way to go."

"But what about the messages the girl received? We should work on that too," says Chris.

"Of course," she answers confidently, "But let's figure out things one at a time. Only when we're clear about what happened between Olivia and Peter, may we have more information about Mason Palmer. Also, have any of you found out whether they have two phones?"

Both detectives shake their heads.

"I've checked it out before, but we haven't found yet," Jordan answers.

"That's all right," Dale says, "Just focus on Olivia's case first, especially you, Chris. I need you guys to finish the investigation in one week. Also, I don't want you to talk too much about this case to that girl."

Just then Chris' mobile phone rings.

"Hello, Detective Bambos speaking. Really? Okay. I'll be there very soon."

He quickly grabs his jacket and leaves the office.

12

Joey

I take three days off from work. I'm feeling quite exhausted recently, both physically and mentally. I find it hard to focus, including ignoring my colleagues after they call my name several times, and I always need to read sentences twice. Even in the evenings after work, I spend a lot of time lying on the bed but with my eyes staring at the ceiling without being asleep. The feeling is almost like there is someone knocking at my head and never stopping. This almost breaks me.

I need to confirm that the news I saw last time was related to Mason, and I expect Olivia is also the one who got involved to link them together. I haven't received any more messages from Chris. I'm not surprised. Detectives are always busy, and I can't ask him to tell me any details from the case, even though he is Vinny's friend.

But what else can I do if I want to dig around more? I'm not interested in who sent me the unknown messages now, but I wonder why he was sending them. If he was truly referring to Mason, my big brother, then

I must figure out what exactly happened several years ago, because this must be linked to something which affects me at present. Otherwise, why was he making me pay attention to something that happened before I was born?

I lie down on the sofa, earphones on. Music does not help me now. I want to talk to someone, but everyone else is at work now: Vinny, Ava, Emily and Ethan. I feel a bit guilty for calling sick today without doing anything at home after breakfast.

Finally, I decide to go out for a walk. I don't need my bag, my laptop or the access card to my workplace. Just myself, my own mind. My earphones are still on, so I almost open the main door without looking outside. Just after I turn around to lock the door, I feel a hand on my shoulder.

I scream and almost jump.

"It's me, it's me, Joey, you idiot." Vinny also looks surprised and then begins to laugh. "What are you doing?"

"Oh my God," I scream, even though I see who it is, "You almost scared me to death! How dare you ask me what I'm doing. That's what I should be asking you."

"Calm down, girl," he answers with a naughty smile, "I'm on leave today from work and yesterday your cousin told me you were going to call in sick at work. So, I came here to check on you."

"Go away. Don't make me feel more guilty." I hit him and laugh. "I'm just going for a walk. No one is talking to me. So bored."

"Why not come to my house?" he suggests and looks at me sincerely. "I have some whiskey in my house, and I've cooked some pasta and mushroom soup. At uni it was always you to cook for me, now it's my turn. I also bought the new FIFA, and we can play. Sound good?"

I say yes without even considering it. I always feel relieved when I see him. Any time.

We cross the road and walk side by side on Abingdon Road. He is wearing a grey T-shirt, a pair of cargo trousers with Air Jordan sneakers. He suddenly notices I'm staring at him.

"You all right? Is it because I'm too handsome?"

"You're so shameless."

"Ahh, don't say that." He gives me a wink. "I'm glad you're happy to come with me. At first, I thought you wouldn't."

"Why?"

"You said you were exhausted."

"But that's not because of you. That's because of work, and…"

"I know." He doesn't look at me, but his words are serious.

We keep silent for the next few minutes until we arrive at his house. It's not far away from my place, just a fifteen-minute walk. I haven't been to his place for a long time since I started my job. It's quite different from the time when we were at uni. During those days I didn't know many people, and he was my best friend. He still is. But now my time is split by too many unrelated people. And sometimes I just want to go home after a tiring day.

His dog John scratches my trousers and almost jumps to my shoulder when I step in the house.

"John, sit!"

The puppy sits without moving.

"I think you are his real master." Vinny looks speechlessly. "Black tea with soy milk?"

"That would be great." I sit on the sofa and smile. "A lot of soy milk."

"You are a weirdo. I've never seen someone who wants so much milk in their tea. But I've gotten used to it."

He pours almost half a cup of soy milk in my teacup, puts a spoon in it and passes the cup to me. "Be careful. Everything else is ready. I'll bring the food here."

He turns around and steps into the kitchen. I can see him from where I'm sitting, opposite the kitchen, so I can see him turning his back to me, bending and using the fork to transfer something from the pot to two plates. I can tell he's still not very used to the kitchen. However, it has been ages since I felt so relaxed, to stay with someone I one hundred percent trust. I take out my phone and take a picture of his back secretly. The sunshine makes his hair look even more stunning. Just then, he puts the food in front of me, with some cream of mushroom soup.

"I'll bring mine as well."

"It looks yummy. You know what I love."

"Try this. Now, is it good?" He looks very excited but also a bit nervous, expecting me to tell him it tastes good.

"I'm surprised, Vinny. Are you sure this is made by yourself?" I try a bit of the tomato-flavoured pasta and give my comments.

"Of course. You underestimate me too much, Joey." He laughs like a child, and then turns to a more serious tone. "I'm happy that you like it. Ahh, shit. I forgot about the football match." He checks his mobile phone. "Fine. It's already finished. Never mind."

We keep silent for a few seconds, enjoying the lunch. I can tell he's starving. He almost finishes his soup while I only finish about half. To be honest, I never feel embarrassed when I spend time with him even without saying anything. We are too familiar with each other. However, I find it a bit odd today as I feel like he wants to tell me something. He's quiet just because he wants to choose the right time to tell me. I'm not sure what it is.

"Are you sure you're all right?"

"Yes."

I stare at him with a confused look. "Do you have something to tell me?"

"Actually, yes." He takes a sip of the soup. "Chris told me his partner contacted the police in Scotland, and it's confirmed that one of the victims was Mason Palmer. So, it was your big brother."

I don't respond. This is what I expected.

"The other victim was Peter Wilson's son, Tracy," he continues, "The police also tried to contact George Woods High School, but they checked and they never had a student in 2000 called Olivia Stretford. No records."

"Nothing else?"

He shrugs.

What? I think. *Nothing related to her? How could that be possible?*

"I was struggling to decide whether I needed to tell you." Vinny sighs. "Now the police won't link this case to the messages you received, I'm afraid. They found a lot of warning notes in Olivia's house, which proves that she got stalked. They're now looking at CCTV around Olivia's house on that morning to look for more evidence. But if they do prove the victim pretended to be a delivery man, they'll end this case and judge it as self-defence."

"I don't believe that."

"I know." He rubs my hair gently, speaking slowly. "What happened recently is in a mess. I'm sorry, Joey."

"Not your fault." I smile back, trying not to look disappointed. "We did all we could do. Maybe the police will get more clues. I lost almost my whole family, and I just want to figure out what happened to them."

"We'll see. I promise I'll let you know anything else if I get more news."

"Thank you for telling me."

"Not at all," he answers, "Oh, I almost forgot about one thing!"

"What's that?"

"Chris also told me on the phone that Mason Palmer's parents were both doctors in Chalmers Centre. They tried to save their son, but they failed."

13

"Where did you go today?" Ethan says, hearing the door open. "Your phone was not responding, and today Ava said a young detective came looking for you."

"I went to Vinny's. I had dinner with him. Sorry, I forgot to tell you," Joey replies, showing her mobile phone, "My phone died. I need a charger."

"Don't worry. Is everything ok?" Ethan smiles softly, handing her an iPhone charger.

"Yes," she answers without looking at her uncle.

Emily walks out from her room as soon as she hears her niece's voice.

"What the hell? A detective?" She stares at Joey with a serious tone, "Was he the guy with Vincent last time? But you didn't tell us anything about this."

Joey is surprised by her aunt's attitude. She was usually very caring and calm. Joey never saw her shouting at anyone or being bossy.

What can she tell her? Say she got a weird message from an unknown number? Sounds ridiculous. She also doesn't want to tell them about it, because her aunt and uncle would be worried if they heard news about Joshua. She still remembers how they struggled with their life after they kept losing important people: her parents, her twin brother... And now she knows something happened to her big brother too. If she asks her aunt about him, maybe she will know something. But is asking them better than reminding them and making them feel bad?

"I'm fine. He was looking for me just because I might have witnessed something related to an accident," she lies, scratching her neck, "Nothing really happened."

"You sure?" Emily looks unconvinced, "Then what did you say to him?"

"I just said what I saw and what I remembered. That's it," she replies.

"Why did you get involved? Just say you don't know anything. It's none of your business."

"Why not? It could be helpful for the investigation." Joey is confused. "It won't do any harm."

"Okay," her aunt says, suddenly increasing her voice, "But how could you be sure you would be safe if you said something? Do you know there is something called witness protection?"

"Don't push her too much, love," Ethan suddenly says, "She looks tired. She needs some space."

"But…"

He shakes his head, giving a "don't continue" gesture to his wife.

"Joey, go and eat something. Your aunt is just worried about you. Don't be upset about that. You know what you're doing. I trust you." Ethan gives her a comforting smile.

Her aunt is still going to say something, but finally she quits.

Just then, Ava appears in the living room.

"What's going on?" She looks between her parents and cousin, "You're back, Joey."

Even before she figures out what's going on, her parents have already stepped back into their room without answering her.

"Are you okay?"

"I'm fine. Don't worry, just tired," Joey replies, giving her a gesture to come to her room.

"Well, I don't know how to describe what happened." Joey closes the door and shrugs. "Maybe I'm just overreacting. But don't tell your parents."

"I won't. Trust me."

"One thing. I'm really curious. Did you know I had a big brother before I was born?"

"Yes," Ava answers, "But how did you know? I never saw him, but my mum talked about him before. She said he bullied his classmate at high school, and then one day that boy brought a hammer to hit back. Your brother then got badly injured, but that boy also got pushed hard and hit his head on a desk corner. Finally, they both passed away. That's all my mum told me. She told me not to tell you. Why are you asking this?"

"That boy's father was accidently killed a few days ago."

"What? I beg your pardon?"

"The detective told me he was stalking a lady. He pretended to be a delivery man in the morning and knocked at her door. However, he didn't expect the lady to get a knife to defend herself."

"I see. So, it was an accident?"

"Probably yes." Joey shrugs. "But the investigation is still carrying on, checking some details. To be honest, I don't think it was an accident."

"Did anything else happen?"

"No. Well... yes," Joey murmurs, "But why are you asking?"

Joey notices a little surprise appear on Ava's face, but it disappears quickly.

"Well, nothing. I'm asking because I wonder how you know these things. How did you know the relationship between this victim and your brother's case? That's a lot of information, you know."

This answer made sense. Joey smiles and laughs at herself. Maybe she was becoming oversensitive. How could she not trust Ava, her beautiful, understanding cousin?

"Because I received a weird message," Joey continues. "It said my brother's death was not an accident. But do you remember previously your mum mentioned I had a big brother before I was born?"

"One second," Ava interrupts, "Which brother?"

"That's the question. You get it. And the day after I received this message, the stalker was killed."

"My God. What the hell? It sounds so scary," Ava says, "How much do you know about your big brother? My mum told me he died almost the same year you were born."

"To be honest, I almost forgot about that," Joey replies, "But a few days ago I remembered my parents took Joshua and me to his grave when we were kids. I still remember that."

"Well, what's going on is just a bit messy."

The two girls keep silent for a few seconds. Joey feels too tired to share her other opinions with her cousin anymore. Yesterday what Vincent told her made her become suspicious. She didn't expect her parents to be the ones trying to save their own child, her big brother. Did anything else happen in the hospital? She can't imagine how they were feeling at that moment, perhaps much more pain than the moment when she almost lost her whole family. She suddenly feels ashamed of herself. She knows too little about what happened to her family.

"Joey, I know what you're feeling now," Ava says, breaking the silence, "But let's hold on a bit. I guess things will be much clearer after the investigation. Don't overthink. There's almost nothing you can do now."

"You're right." Joey sighs. "Fine. Let's stop this topic. I'll get some ice cream now." She stands up from the bed and opens the door.

Her uncle is in the kitchen, making some hot chocolate. He sees her coming out and quickly adds marshmallows to the hot chocolate, giving the cup to her.

"Be careful. It's hot," he says, "Your aunt asked me to make this for you. She felt sorry about what she said just now."

"Not at all." Joey smiles. "It was me that made you worry. Tell her I'm fine."

She notices her uncle looks much more relieved after he hears this.

14

Jordan and Chris stare at the computer screen with a blurred video. It's still clear that it's CCTV footage of the opposite of Olivia Stretford's house in the early morning. This angle doesn't show Olivia's main door, but it shows the front pavement next to the road. It's a deserted road. Even a leaf could be noticed if it fell. There are a few motorcycles, with a man who is walking his dog. Nothing relevant appears at this point.

"It's ten past eight," Jordan complains, "No one is approaching the house."

"Be patient, bro," Chris replies, "It might not be exactly 8 a.m."

Just after he says this, a truck stops in front of the house coming from the right direction, which just blocks the vision of the entry of the pavement. What they can see is the grey part of the truck, and it seems like there is someone opening the door from the driver's seat. However, the driver's side is not facing the CCTV camera, so there is no way to see what this person looked like and whether it was Peter Wilson.

"Shit," Jordan murmurs, "Are you sure there aren't any other CCTV cameras around here?"

"Nope. I've checked. This one was the best to show what was around her house," Chris says, "But anyway, I think we can still get some clues from this footage."

"Are you joking? I can't see anything here."

"Well, we still need to find ways to check if this driver was Peter Wilson. I think it was," Chris answers, "But at least we know that Olivia is not lying about this. Also, there was only one person in the truck…"

"Chris!" Laura's voice suddenly calls out in the office, "There's someone who would like to speak to you. He says he's Olivia's neighbour, and he might have seen the delivery man."

"Okay. Thanks, Laura. I'll come now." He gives a gesture to Jordan to tell him to come too.

They follow Laura to a small room. A man is already waiting there. He looks around forty with thick whiskers, not very tall, but fit.

"Hello," Chris greets him and offers his hand, "I am Detective Bambos. Thank you for coming, sir. Laura told me about you when she started the investigation. I hear that you have something to report. Did you remember any details?"

"Yes," the man replies, with a slow but strong voice, "I live just beside that lady. Of course, I forgot her name. But I saw a man that early morning. I'm not sure whether he was the one you were trying to work out."

"I see. Sorry, may I have your name please?"

"Patrick Stones," he says, then continues, "I'm a bit ashamed to say, but the lady was gorgeous, and sometimes I met her when she finished work. And the window of my kitchen is just facing her main door. So…"

The two detectives smile but do not say anything. Obviously, they are more interested in what he saw that day.

"Yes, and on that morning, after I got up, I was washing my cup in the kitchen. I heard some footsteps approaching her main door, so I had a look. Then I saw a man standing in front of her door and knocking."

"What time was that?"

"I think it was some time past eight."

"Did you see the man's face?"

"No, detective. He was not facing me. Also, there's a wooden fence between my house and her house. As you can see, I'm not tall enough. I only noticed he was wearing a hat and a black shirt."

The two detectives look at each other at the same time.

"One second," Chris asks, "You mentioned the door opened. Did the lady open the door for him?"

"Yes, I think so." The man slows down his words and begins to remember, "Well, I can't say a hundred percent as the man blocked my vision, so I'm not sure if it was her who opened the door for him, and I didn't hear her saying anything."

"Okay. It makes sense," Chris replies, making some notes quickly.

"Did you see anything else? Like whether he was carrying something?" Jordan asks.

"Oh yes! That's what I forgot to say as I didn't really see him, but when the door was open, he bent over for a few seconds, you know, looked like he was carrying a box, sort of."

"What about after? Did you see the man leaving?"

"No. Actually, after I saw that, I left my house to catch the bus, so I'm not sure when he left."

"Good." Chris smiles. "The last question, did you see any friends or partners of this lady?"

"No, I never saw anyone coming to her house. This was the first time I saw anyone coming to her."

"Okay. Thank you, Mr Stones. Your information will be helpful for us to figure out what happened."

The two detectives went back to the office after the short conversation.

"Peter Wilson was wearing a black shirt. It's true. We also found a black hat in Olivia's house." Jordan looks excited.

"No. We still didn't get the whole picture."

"Why?"

"Remember what he said. He only saw the hat and his top. Also that this man might have been carrying something. What do you think he was carrying?"

"What do you mean?"

Just then, a new WhatsApp messages jumps to Chris' screen. It's from Joey.

Hey Chris, my cousin told me that you were looking for me yesterday afternoon. Is there any news you would like to tell me?

He freezes for a moment. He never went to Joey's place yesterday.

15

Joey

I get on the train to Edinburgh Waverley in the early morning.

I suddenly wanted to go to my parents' previous workplace. If I still have time, I would like to have a walk around the area where we used to live. The memory which only belongs to me.

I was too young when I lost my parents, but I remember how Joshua looked when I saw him afterwards in the hospital. For many years, I unbelievably forgot a few moments from that horrible day. I finally remember the tight space in the suitcase, and how I was trying my best not to make any noise, even when I heard Joshua being attacked by the man. I felt guilty as always. If I hadn't opened the door, the man wouldn't have found us. I didn't dare come out to save my brother. However, what's happened recently has made me dig more into my memory. My parents' case was defined as a robbery by the police, because all the money and valuable stuff was gone. However, I could feel the complete hatred from the man instead of a strong desire for money only. After Joshua finally left the hospital after several operations, I mentioned this to him so many times, but he refused to talk about it.

"Forget about that, Joey. I don't know what happened either. The police might be right. No matter what happened and what will happen, it's never your fault." That's what he always said.

Now I find out something which is linked to my parents. They failed to save their son. No matter what else there is, I would like to know as much as I can. If someone in Chalmers Centre knows them, maybe they will tell me something which no one else knew before. What if this is also linked to their death?

It is not a short journey to Edinburgh. I have already told Ava that today one of my colleagues is having a birthday party and I will stay overnight. Of course, it's a lie.

Sitting on the seat, I feel my brain is not so stressed like the last few days, and I'm even stepping into some unknown places in my sleep until I'm woken up by the broadcast from the train. I can't believe I fell asleep for some time.

"We will soon arrive at Edinburgh Waverly. The train will terminate here."

The door opens after a few minutes, with a cooler atmosphere outside.

I'm back.

I go upstairs from the train station and to the exit on Princes Street. I always used to go that way. After a few minutes' walk, I see the Scott Monument and the bright Princes Street Gardens. Everything is like usual: cafes, high-street brands, TK Maxx. It's a shame I'm not here to travel or go shopping. I need to get a bus to my destination.

It's not hard to get there. No more than twenty minutes by bus. There haven't been many big changes around here, which enables me to follow my memories from childhood. There are several different clinical centres around, and it is the square-shaped building, which is called Lauriston Building, that my parents used to work in. Its shape is a typical square-shaped structure, surrounded by a few stairs and a parking area. It doesn't take me long to find the entrance. My parents used to work in the emergency department. That was why they never had time to pick us up after school, so they always asked us to come to the hospital to find them and go home together.

There are not many people waiting on the seats. The whole atmosphere looks peaceful and organised. I'm a bit surprised because it used to be very busy. Time can change everything, can't it?

"Hi, good afternoon, are you all right?" A young lady sitting behind the counter notices me.

"Hello." I suddenly feel a bit lost. What can I say? Ask her whether she knew my parents?

She is looking at me continuously, waiting for my response.

"I'm sorry," I reply, "I'm not here to ask for medical help, but I... Have you heard about someone who used to work here fifteen years ago called Dr Sarah Jones?"

Sarah was my mum.

She looks confused and gently shakes her head. "No. I've only worked here for two years, so I have no idea."

"That's all right. But could you help me ask others here to see whether they know her please?"

She exchanges eye contact with another woman sitting in the corner. Both of them shake their heads.

"Look. I have no idea about the person you're looking for. That's a long time ago."

I don't answer them at once. I look around my surroundings, trying to find anyone that matches my limited memory before.

"Sorry, if you don't have anything else to ask, you'll have to leave. Next patient please!" She doesn't pay attention to me after she says that.

"Please, does anyone else know?" I don't move, staring at the internal working area.

"Well, this is a hospital. If you want to find someone, call the police," another older lady answers me in an annoyed tone.

They're right. How could I think I would find anything about my parents from fifteen years ago? I must be mad.

"What's going on here?"

When I'm about to leave, a man walks out from a room inside the clinical area. He is in white, looks at least over forty-five, with a pair of glasses and a skinny face.

"Dr Morris, this girl keeps asking whether we know someone called Sarah Jones. But we both have no idea. And she doesn't want to leave," the woman complains.

His emotionless face turns into an incredible expression after he hears my mum's name. "Are you... Are you Dr Palmer's daughter?"

Dad.

I nod gently, as if it's just a simple greeting, but he quickly leaves the enquiry area and asks me to come with him.

"You've grown up, girl." He holds my hands. "I can't believe you're here."

I don't move, staring at him with a confused look. I didn't have a good memory before I was ten. Did I meet him before in the hospital?

"It's normal that you don't remember me." He realises my confusion, beginning to explain. "I was your dad's assistant before. I changed my hairstyle. I'm also wearing glasses now. It's been many years. But I remember you."

"You knew my parents?"

"Of course." He speaks slowly. "I also remember your twin brother. But I forgot his name. How is he?"

"He passed away."

"What? How could that have happened? I'm sorry." He freezes for a few seconds, lowering his head. "You have to be strong. You need to live for them."

Live for them. A lot of people have said this to me. Living is easy. But living for them is hard.

"Why did you come here today? Anything I can help you with?" he finally asks.

"I need to know something about my parents, sir," I answer, "Do you know... I used to have a big brother before I was born..."

His face turns pale, as if reminding him of something really horrible. "You know that?" he murmurs, "Fine. I can tell you what I saw. Let's talk in my office."

I follow him, passing through a corridor, and walk into his office.

"You're not in the emergency department anymore?"

"There is no emergency department now," he answers, "They put me in the ear, nose and throat department not long after your parents passed away. Everything changes."

I don't know what to say at this moment. It suddenly feels unreal. This is the person who worked with my parents before. He knows even more about them than me.

"You asked me about your big brother," he continues, "It was a tragedy. He was only twelve years old. When he was sent here, his head was badly injured. I forget some details... At first your mum didn't know. When she arrived, your dad was doing cardiopulmonary resuscitation continuously for his son. We all knew he was gone. But your dad was like a robot. Finally, someone else had to force him to leave."

"Was there another injured boy?"

"Yes. I can't believe the police also arrived afterwards. Seems like it was the boy's mother. She was crying out why we didn't save her son first."

"Do you mean my parents paid more attention to my big brother instead of the other boy?"

"No, it's not like that." He speeds up his voice. "When the two boys were sent here, your brother was still conscious. He was even calling for your dad, but the other boy was already unconscious. We found out and the other few doctors and me told your dad to focus on his son, and we would save the other boy. However, that boy was already gone. Just then, his mother arrived, realising her son was gone, but she saw your dad still there with your brother. Then she cried, lay on the floor and the police had to drag her outside."

I sit on the sofa, listening to his words as if I'm really seeing all of the scenes. I feel chilly and shiver.

I know my parents had to have blamed themselves for a long time. If I were them, I would always feel like I had failed a child, and this was because I didn't take care of them. But it was not true. In my memory, they always tried their best to spend time with us.

"After that day, your parents were off work for two weeks," he says, "Your dad looked fine, not too bad.

But we all knew he was pretending. Because at that moment, your mum was four months pregnant. He needed to be by her side."

He looks at me with a comforting look.

"Everyone was worrying about your mum. I can't imagine how she experienced the trauma and still gave birth to you. Just one month before you were born, that boy's mother came to the hospital and threatened her. She was crying for her to give her son back to her."

"I guess she thought my parents didn't save her son because they put their child first," I say.

"Yes, she did. The police must have told her afterwards. That's why. But it's never anyone's fault."

"Did any of you see the boy's father?" I ask.

"Yes, but he was a very considerate man." He finally smiles. "We saw him when he was persuading his wife to go home instead of giving your parents trouble. He kept saying, 'Tracy is gone. It's no one's fault'."

"Do you remember what his father looked like?"

"Umm, not really. Sorry. I only remember he was white, not very tall, with a beard. Did something happen?"

Yes. That considerate man you mentioned is dead. And it seems like he was stalking a lady for a long time, I think.

"It's fine if you don't want to say." He gently puts his hand on my shoulder. "Be strong. I feel like you might have already gotten some information from your big brother's case." He stares at me for a few seconds. "I don't know if that matters to you. Others might tell you that your brother bullied that boy. Don't listen to them. It's not true."

16

"I think it's almost here." Chris is sitting in the driver's seat, staring at Google Maps. "But where is it?"

"Over there. Come on, Chris. You're such a nerd." Jordan laughs. His partner was always perfect except for his bad sense of direction. He also couldn't wait to get out of the car as they had been driving for several hours from Oxford to Edinburgh. However, he really admires his partner's act.

They finally stop in front of the main entrance to George Wood High School.

Chris quickly makes a call, and a man appears behind the gate and greets them after a few minutes. He looks around fifty years old, in a casual grey jumper with long hair tied up.

"Hello, detectives." He offers his hand. "My name is Lucas. Arthur told me everything, and I'm happy to answer what you would like to know about the case as I was their class teacher. I've been working here for twenty-five years since I graduated."

"Nice to meet you," Chris replies, "This is my partner, Jordan. That would be great. Do you still have the yearbook for that year?"

"Yes. I found it for you. We're all set. Let's talk inside."

They follow Lucas to the campus, facing the brown main building. It's still lesson time, so there are no pupils around them.

"This is my office. Please take any seats you like."

"Thank you, Lucas. It's such a beautiful campus, isn't it?"

"Yes, it is. I love the pupils and it's a nice place to work," Lucas answers, "Right. I heard from Arthur that you would like to know details from that school bullying case that happened in 2000. Is that right?"

"Yes. The first thing I would like to confirm is," Chris says, showing him the photo of Olivia Stretford, "Do you know this lady? Or in other words, do you know whether this person studied here before?"

Lucas takes the photo and stares at it for a few seconds. "No. I don't think so. At least she was not in my class. But maybe we could check together in the yearbook to see whether she was here. The yearbook has all the students' photos."

"Sounds good. It's very important to us."

Lucas stands up, bringing a blue hard-cover file from his shelf to the desk. He opens the yearbook, turning the pages continuously, until he reaches one page with several photos and turns it to the two young men. His finger points to one of the photos which belongs to a boy. "This was one of the two teenagers, Mason Palmer."

Chris stares at the chestnut hair of the boy, which reminds him of another similar face at once. "They looked like each other."

Then their attention is taken by another photo.

"This was the other boy, Tracy Wilson."

"Do you know the reason why they were bullied?" Chris asks.

"No. Actually, they weren't bullied by other students," Lucas replies, "Mason was an indifferent type. Not many students wanted to play with him, so his personality was a bit odd. On that day, several students saw that he had an argument with Tracy, but no one saw who carried the hammer. Both of them got badly injured."

"Really? So there were several students who were witnesses?" Jordan says.

"Yes." Lucas moves his attention to the photos again without looking at them. "But as for the photo you showed me just now... well, seems like she didn't study here, I'm afraid."

"That's all right." Chris smiles. "Don't worry. What about this guy?" He takes out another photo.

"Oh, I know him, of course. He's Tracy's father, Peter." Lucas' eyes brighten for a few seconds. "He is a good man, very considerate. I'm sorry for what he experienced. Do you guys know Mason's parents were both doctors? I heard they tried to save their son first, and Peter's wife was almost mad about that, but even then, he still tried to persuade his wife to calm down."

Chris nods, quickly making some notes in his little notebook.

"May I ask, has something happened to Peter?" Lucas asks.

"Sorry, Lucas. We can't talk about cases with you at the moment. But we will contact you again if we need more information," Chris apologises and provides his card. "Also, Lucas, could you try to remember whether you saw this lady before? You don't need to answer me now, but if you remember anything related, call me at any time."

"No problem. I will try, detective."

"Final question," Chris continues, "You just mentioned several students witnessed this case. Do you have their names?"

"Umm, I can't remember." Lucas scratches his head. "They were also in my class, of course, but the news spread out from the students. I don't know who exactly said what."

"Okay," Chris says, "May I take a photo of this page of photos?"

Lucas hesitates for a second. "Yes, of course. Go ahead."

Both detectives stand up. "Thank you for your help, Lucas. We'll be in touch."

They say goodbye then leave.

"What do you think, Chris?"

"I have no idea now," Chris says in an emotionless tone, "We won't get a full picture if we can't find a connection between Olivia and Peter. I just took the student photos of that page with their names. Tell Laura to pick a few of them and find their contact numbers and basic information."

"Okay. But I'm hungry. I haven't had any food in a few hours," Jordan complains.

"Same." Chris laughs, looking for his car keys. "I know there was a good restaurant around here."

As Jordan opens the car door, he suddenly points to the opposite road. "Is that Joey? The girl who said she received the weird message?"

17

"Miss Stretford, your injuries are much better now. You can leave the hospital and go home today or tomorrow." With caring eyes, the nurse pours a cup of water for Olivia, and helps her to sit up in bed. "You look much better."

"Thanks," she replies simply, trying to move her injured leg. It's still swollen and wrapped, but at least much better than before. "How long will that take to completely recover?"

"It's different for different people. But for you I would say, one to two months," the nurse answers in a comforting tone. "Don't worry. It won't produce big scars. By the way, the detective who visited you a few days ago asked about your situation. He asked us to take good care of you."

She shrugs. No, she was not taken care of. She only wants to be taken care of by one person.

Now she could go home. But where? She didn't have anywhere else to go. Yesterday she received a call from Chris, and he told her that they still had to further investigate her house for two to three days, so they had booked her a hotel room just five minutes' walk from the hospital. This caring detective said if she had nowhere to stay then she should text him and he would come and help her to check in.

Sounded like a good idea, but she didn't feel good. She did have a home. She could just go to her mum's house. No, that was not home, just a house. She never received any calls or messages from her mum, but she was pretty sure the police had contacted her.

"I've never been your choice, Mum," she says to herself.

In her childhood, she used to try to figure out why her parents didn't even pay a little bit of attention to her. One day, she got the answer from her big sister. She was always arrogant due to the attitude from their parents.

"It's your fault Mum has to work so hard."

This explanation was enough for her to figure out why. But what else could she do? She helped with the housework at home, did part-time jobs to buy gifts for her family when she was only a teenager, and never asked for anything. But she was still regarded as a tool to look after her sister, who never deserved care and love.

No, she couldn't go to her mother's.

Finally, she picks up her phone on the small table beside her bed and dials Chris' number. She usually hates police and detectives, as she doesn't like their cold eye contact, emotionless words and useless official tone. But this man was different. He was polite, caring and sympathetic. He didn't judge her. He didn't force her to talk. He didn't stress her. He was just like a friend who was trying to figure out what happened to her. This changed her usual impression on cops.

"Sorry, the number you dialled is unavailable."

"Maybe he is busy." She's not surprised. Instead, she sends a text message to him saying she would like to leave the hospital and move to the hotel he had arranged for her.

After she does this, she lies down again in the bed. Suddenly she sits up again, trying to grab her handbag under the bed. Her hand is searching for something. There it is. The burner phone.

An unread message.

Liv, are you all right? Please reply. I will come and see you.

What? You can't. How can you come here? she thinks.

Just then, the door opens. A male nurse steps into the room and closes the door. No, it's not a nurse.

"Oh my God, Mike, why are you here? I just saw your message, but why? It's so risky." She almost jumps, grabbing the man's arm.

The man makes a shushing gesture to her, making sure there is no one coming close to the room.

"But I'm worried about you." He lowers his voice. "Let me have a look." He touches her shoulder, trying to examine her.

She doesn't refuse his care. He holds her shoulder and then gives her a tight hug, as if he was scared to lose her. He cups her face in his hands and kisses her. She closes her eyes, feeling his temperature passing through his hand to his tongue, and then to her body.

"How did you get the white coat?"

"Never mind that. I always have my way." He winks at her. "When are you leaving hospital?"

"Today or tomorrow," she answers, and then becomes less certain, "There was a detective who visited me. I can't go back to my place now, but they arranged a hotel for me."

"Are you going to go?"

"I don't have any other choice." Her gaze stays on him, seeking his opinion.

"I know." He takes her hand. "I'm sorry. But trust me, it'll be over. But get in touch, okay?" He looks at her burner phone.

Just then, they hear someone knocking at the door.

"Miss Stretford, may I come in?"

"You have to hide!"

Before the doctor twists the door handle, she quickly drops her cup to the floor.

"Are you all right? I just heard a big noise in your room."

"Well, don't worry, doctor," she answers, "I just wanted to grab my cup from the bag. But it dropped. Don't worry."

Her bag just blocks the arm under the bed.

18

The man sitting on the sofa is trying his best not to keep staring at the girl's face. The chestnut hair, the heavy eyebrows, the round nose tip. All of these remind him of his previous classmate in junior high school. They are too similar to be true.

Then he was right. These two detectives are here because of that case, otherwise they would not have asked him which high school he went to.

"Okay. Thank you, Lorenzo." Jordan exchanges eye contact with Chris. "Do you still remember the case that happened between two of your classmates?"

Here it is.

"Yes, yes," he replies, repeating his words, "I'm sorry for what happened to them. But I'm not sure why they were... fighting with each other."

"That's all right. Don't worry. But we just visited your previous class teacher, Lucas Harris. He told us you were one of the witnesses. Tell us what you saw."

He rubs his hands, finally coming out with three words. "I can't remember."

"I'll get to the point straight away," Chris suddenly says, "Something happened to one of the case-related personnel, and we need to check anything that could be useful. Nothing will happen to you, sir. But what you tell us will be very important."

Lorenzo looks at Joey again. She isn't staring at him. Instead, she appears calm, like a sculpture. No emotion can be identified on her face.

"Well, what I saw was Mason carried a hammer to hit Tracy, and then they both fell on the floor. Then they were both sent to the hospital. There were also other students who saw that, but when I arrived, that was all I saw."

"How was your relationship with them?"

"To be honest, I liked Mason." The man bit his lip. "He was very quiet, but he was a good guy. I think he must have had a reason to behave like that. But I have no idea."

"What about Tracy then?"

"Umm... he was a top student in our class." Lorenzo scratches his head, "Almost every teacher liked him. But I didn't talk to him very much."

"Another quick check," Chris asks, "Was there a student called Olivia in your class or someone you know called that?"

"No," Lorenzo answers immediately, but he continues, "One second, I know there was a girl who was on our campus football team called Olivia. But I never talked to her before."

"Is this her?" Like he did before with Lucas, Jordan takes out Olivia's photo.

"No. I've never seen anyone who looks like that." Lorenzo shakes his head. "I'm sorry."

"That's all right," Chris answers, "We're trying to figure out whether she was related to this case. Could you think about anything else weird at that moment?"

Lorenzo touches his chin, which looks like he's digging in his mind. Apparently, it's not easy for him.

"Take your time. Any tiny thing might be important."

He keeps silent for a few minutes. Should he tell them or not?

"I can't remember anything that I thought was a bit off, detective," he finally says, looking like he made a big decision, "But I need to confess. I don't know why they fought with each other, but I did see Tracy bullying a girl before."

"How?"

"He insulted her many times. He said she looked like a toad, an ugly monster, with low intelligence.

There was also a time he tried to trip her when she was running in PE class." His voice goes lower and lower as he says these things. However, he feels much more relieved.

"Did your other classmates know this as well?" Chris looks unsurprised.

"Yes, but most of us ignored it... That girl had a rare skin disease with many rashes on her face, and she rarely spoke to anyone. Almost no one cared about her. I remember her name was Ellie, if I'm right."

"Then why do you think this is related to this case?"

"Because Mason was the only person who tried to help her. He tried to comfort her and asked her to ignore the bad words."

"So, you think this might be the reason why he argued with Tracy?"

"Yes, and because of that, our class teacher, Lucas, hated Mason so much. I think he knew everything that happened in the class, but he stopped us telling anything to the police or media. Some of us were interviewed a few times by the police, and a girl was trying to tell them about how Tracy bullied Ellie, but then she suddenly changed the story afterwards. She claimed she wasn't sure."

"That's dodgy, isn't it?" Jordan looks at Chris. "What was her name?"

"Rebecca. Wait, you just asked me about someone called Olivia, right? It might be irrelevant, but I remember once I heard Rebecca having a call, and she mentioned one name several times: Livvy."

"Livvy? Right..." Chris takes out his phone and shows Lorenzo the pictures of the yearbook. "Could you please show me the two girls you just mentioned, Mr James?"

Lorenzo hesitates to take the phone and carefully examines the photos by scrolling through them. He isn't sure whether he can still identify their younger faces. Almost everyone look different when they're fifteen, but he still notices himself first: the boy wearing glasses with freckles on his face. How time flies. He doesn't pay too much attention to himself. His eyes are flying around the faces to find the ones he was asked to look for.

One second.

"No. They're not here. Sorry, detectives," he finally says, "I almost forgot. Both of them wouldn't be in this yearbook."

19

Joey

I never expected to meet Chris in Edinburgh. But actually, he did what I wanted to do. I feel a bit surprised because if he went to the high school, it means he cares about the anonymous messages I told him about and realises the importance of figuring out the connection between Olivia Stretford and Peter Wilson.

Lorenzo seems to choose to be honest finally. He explains the reason for the absence of the two girls related to Mason's case in the yearbook. Rebecca was sent to the US after the accident happened, while the bullied girl, Ellie, had a one-year gap after it happened due to psychological trauma. I remember Chris said he would investigate if there was anyone called Olivia from the people who Rebecca knew. There's not much I can do right now. However, the moment I heard about my parents again after a few years still made me cry.

Then I think about that message again. It's so confusing I can't stop thinking about it. If it did refer to Mason, his case was absolutely an accident. My parents tried their best to save his life. Or was I actually wrong?

Did the message refer to Joshua? In that case, how could we explain Peter Wilson's relation to the case?

I quit my confusion now as I am already exhausted from work. Now I only want to take a bath and go to bed.

Just then, I hear a new message coming to my phone.

It's Vinny. It's always him.

I'M OUTSIDE.

That's it.

I open the door at once. It's him. He looks pale and exhausted. I smell alcohol.

"Freaking hell. You got drunk?" I say with a surprised look.

He rarely gets drunk. At least from what I know.

He shakes his head, then steps into the house and shuts the door gently.

"Don't worry. I'm fine, Joey. I just wanna spend some time with you. I'll leave in a while."

I hold his arm and we walk into my room together.

"How are you?" he asks.

"I'm all right," I say, handing him a glass of water, "I've had enough for today's work, just chilling."

"I heard from Chris that you went to Edinburgh."

He hesitates a bit. "What were you up to?"

"Well, you know…" I answer, "I just wanted to go to my parents' previous hospital. Mason was sent there to be treated. I can't imagine what they experienced, especially when my mum was already pregnant with us."

"You're still suspicious about your parents' death, aren't you?"

"I don't know if I can trust the police. That message couldn't be tracked. It's very confusing as well. What they can do is limited. Things are in a mess."

"Well, Chris will figure it out. Not only is he my friend, but he's a very sensitive guy and very responsible."

"I hope so." My voice is quite low, without sounding too convinced.

"But you're still trying to figure it out all by yourself." He suddenly raises his voice. "I know you've been concerned since you received that message."

I shrug, ignoring his words. "Now tell me what happened to you, Vinny."

"Nothing really." He looks into my eyes. "I just need a little time to throw away my emotional rubbish. My team leader has been getting so mean recently. He ignores me almost all of the time in team meetings. No matter what I do, he's never satisfied. I don't understand. Why can't people treat others nicely, Joey?"

"It happens, Vinny. I fully get it." I grab his hand. "We can't ensure how people treat us. But we need to still be ourselves."

"You're right." He lowers his head. "I'm also worried about you. Look, sometimes I imagine if I had experienced what you did, I wouldn't be as strong as you. But I just... I just want to protect you more. I want to do anything that I can to help."

"You've already done that, Vinny."

"No, I haven't. I didn't even know you went to Edinburgh. You should've called me and I would have gone with you."

"Sorry. I just didn't want you to worry about me."

"I don't want to hear it." He raises his voice, but still in a gentle, yet emotional tone. "You don't need to figure it out all by yourself. I want to be a big part of your life. I love you, Joey. I'm serious."

20

Chris almost rushes to the police station.

"Hello?" He appears in front of Dale's office. He is surprised to see Jordan, Laura and Dale are all there. "What the hell happened to Lucas?"

Dale nods slightly, takes a photo from her desk and passes it to Chris. "Here you are. The body was in his bedroom. It was found by one of his colleagues." She stops for a few seconds, then continues. "We have now determined he died of cyanide poisoning."

"What else?"

"I have investigated his social relationship," Laura replies, "He was single, never married, and he lived alone. I also checked with his landlord and credit. No problems at all. Very quiet guy. No signs of a struggle in his house. So probably suicide. But, of course, the possibility of homicide was not completely ruled out."

"It's only two days…" Jordan murmurs, "Since we interviewed him."

"What about the two I told you to look at?" Chris turns to Laura and asks.

"Well, I looked at that yesterday. But they can't be related to their class teacher's case." Laura shakes her head and seems to realise what her favourite detective is thinking. "Rebecca Bryant wasn't even in the UK. I contacted her mum and she said she has been in the US since she was a teenager. She doesn't come back very often. The last time she was back in the UK was nine months ago. For Ellie Lambert, she had a gap year during junior high school, and then she moved to Glasgow to work. I tracked her record for that evening. She was in Glasgow. Of course, you can check if you want. I've noted down their contact information."

"Nah, that's fine if you've confirmed." Chris doesn't look at her but looks convinced. "Both of them didn't show in the yearbook as they left before they graduated. Their previous classmate also said that."

"So, it's suicide, isn't it?" Jordan looks impatiently. "He knew that we would interview his previous students and find out the truth. Then he felt guilty about pushing out his student and banning theming from telling the truth."

"Wait a minute, all of you," Dale suddenly opens her mouth, "Let's get to each point one by one. First, you guys went to Edinburgh to find out if there was any connection between Peter Wilson and Olivia Stretford. Right? How's that going?"

"There wasn't a definite answer, ma'am," Chris answers, "Rebecca Bryant might have connections with someone called Olivia. But Olivia is a common name, so we need to look into that later."

"Then why are you so insistent on checking this?"

"Because this could help us figure out how much we can believe about Olivia's self-defence claim. If she has any motive to kill Peter Wilson, then that unknown message might be true. It's obvious that the sender predicted something would happen in advance, no matter who he is."

"But there's something I don't quite understand, Chris." Dale looks confused. "I remember you told me that the girl had two brothers. How can you be sure which one the sender is talking about?"

"We're not sure," Chris replies, "Joey must be thinking about that too. But she noticed that news article first and we happened to find out it was related to Peter Wilson and her big brother. At this point, I would say, no matter which one, this campus bullying case is the key to the puzzle, especially when Joey's parents were also the doctors who tried to save the two boys."

"You must be joking."

"That's why we're serious about what exactly happened in 2000, ma'am."

Chris doesn't tell her they saw Joey in Edinburgh on that day. He doesn't tell her that Joey didn't believe her parents' death was just a robbery. He doesn't want to make it more complex at the moment as the first question they have to answer is to find out if there could be a possible link between Olivia and the bullying case. She was the key. Everything was just happening too quickly for him to react.

Everything started from that message.

"By the way," Dale says, suddenly facing Laura, "Still no location tracked for that WhatsApp number?"

"No, ma'am."

"But what do we say to the public and the media about Olivia's case? This community is usually very safe. You know, people begin to panic."

"Just tell the facts," Chris says firmly, "Self-defence from a stalker. Nothing needs to worry them. It's true right now. If we keep hiding, it will only bring us trouble."

"By the way, how is Olivia? Did she leave the hospital?"

"Yes. We asked the doctor to send her to the hotel that we arranged for her. We've asked them to supervise her."

"Great." Dale nods. "Then what are you guys up to next?"

"To be honest," Chris says, "I'd like to go to Olivia's house to investigate again. There might be something we ignored before. Just in case."

"We might need to contact Lucas' family members or friends to know more about his life," Jordan adds, "If he did end his own life, I don't think it's only because he was unfair to a previous student. There might be other reasons."

"Great call." Chris gives him a smile. "Also, Laura..." He suddenly hits his own head. "You know Joey, right? I need more help from you to look into her family members, especially her cousin, Ava."

The other three stare at him with a surprised look.

"Last week Joey called me and asked why I visited her house. But I never did."

"So, her cousin told her you did?"

"Oops." Jordan knits his brows. "That's confusing. Why would she do that? If she knew Joey was contacting you, then she should have known that Joey would get back to you and confirm with you. There was no point in lying, unless..."

"Unless she lied just to make us pay attention to her, or someone who was close to her," Chris says.

21

Joey

I said yes to Vinny that evening. We kissed for the first time and said good night to each other. Then he left the house.

I'm in love now. Everything happened so quickly. To be honest, I had gotten used to the feeling I felt when he stayed with me, but I always failed to understand if it could be a relationship. But now he's said it, I have no reason to refuse. We both care about each other. But I'm not ready for living together or sex as I've never been in a relationship before. I need more time.

I haven't heard from Chris for so many days. I tried to call him this afternoon but the call went directly to voicemail.

Suddenly my phone is ringing. It's Chris' number.

"It's me," he speaks as soon as I pick up the phone. "Sorry, I was in a meeting."

"It's ok," I say, "I just wondered if there was anything new about Olivia. You don't need to tell me anything. But I really would like to know, if that's possible."

"Well, Joey... actually that's why I'm calling you now," he says, with some background noise which sounds like a place where everyone is on the phone. "You might be upset about this, but we've stopped the investigation on that point for now."

"Oh," I say, and allow myself a few seconds of respite, "How come?"

I hear him taking a deep breath. "We did find a connection. Olivia is Rebecca's half-sister. She was only a few months older than her."

I doubt my ears. I had thought about a few possibilities, including that the police had found nothing and gave up, even that Olivia was also in the same high school but not the same grade as Mason. But did that make sense? And if so, why did they stop the investigation?

"I know what you're thinking," he continues, "Olivia's biological father divorced her mum when she was only a few weeks old, and her mother got married to her stepdad just after that. Sorry, we didn't even notice that at the very beginning. Her mother was very cold, and she didn't tell us anything. However, we lack evidence to show Olivia knew what happened to Mason and Tracy. She also didn't go to the same high school as her half-sister. She seldom got in touch with her family after she was sixteen."

That's why her last name is not the same as Rebecca's.

I suddenly feel bad for her. I can't imagine a child never receiving attention. Maybe that was the reason why she didn't contact them.

"The clues were all suspended, I'm afraid. As for the message you received, we won't be able to find out who the sender was, especially if that person doesn't do it again."

"Where is Olivia now?" I ask.

"The investigation has now finished, so she was allowed back to her house," he answers, "We interviewed her again and she admitted she had a half-sister. As I mentioned, she didn't have any extra information that helped us. What we had was only the evidence that Peter Wilson was stalking her."

"I understand." This is the only thing I can say at the moment. Everything looked like it was making sense. It could be that the stalking was just a coincidence. As for the message, it could be a prank or it didn't refer to Mason. I remember Lorenzo did mention that Rebecca tried to claim Tracy Wilson was bullying another girl called Ellie for a long time. Could that be the reason Peter Wilson was targeting Olivia because her sister was trying to accuse his son? But if that's true, he was absolutely a crazy person who tried to blame everything on someone else. But almost everyone said he behaved well.

"So, what's next?" he asks.

"Next?" I'm a bit confused. I'm still expecting too much from him. "Well, just going back to normal life…"

"I hope you hold on a bit," he interrupts my words, but pauses a few seconds as well. "It doesn't mean that I don't care about this anymore. I will see. You know, sometimes things don't come together immediately."

"Agreed. You're always nice to me, thanks," I answer, but not really listening to him. My instinct tells me there's still something to this case. If I want to continue, I'll need to ask for some professional services.

"There's another thing I hope you remember." He sounds like he realises I'm not paying attention, "Don't talk about this case to your family. Sorry, what I mean is, your cousin, your aunt and your uncle. Sometimes you may not know."

PART TWO

22

Olivia

I'm really not a bad person, I promise you. I'm not the monster you think I am.

This morning I saw today's newspaper. The police have given up the current investigation about Peter Wilson's case. They claimed I was just acting in self-defence, which was what we expected. Thank God.

Well, let me tell you what happened to me, from the beginning.

Everything started a year ago. That was the first time I saw a weird message on my car when I finished work. It was written in black Sharpie on paper.

TALKING LIKE A LIAR WILL MAKE YOU PAY THE PRICE.

At first, I didn't give a shit as I knew there were some weird people in this country. Maybe they were just hiding somewhere to enjoy the feeling of the prank. However, after one week, an unknown number contacted me.

TALKING LIKE A LIAR WILL MAKE YOU PAY THE PRICE. YOUR SISTER HAS ALREADY TOLD US.

I tried to call back and text back, but no one answered or replied. Of course not. But I felt so sick as he knew my number and that meant he might also know where I live. Although I did have a boyfriend called Mike, he lived quite far away from my place and my workplace. That's why we're still not living together. So I needed to be extremely careful as I was living by myself.

Then I decided to call the police, but they were such idiots. All they told me was that there was not much they could do as I didn't have any clues about who the person was. But the next day, I saw two dead pigeons at the entrance of my house. They were both decapitated and placed together, which looked very creepy. There was also another note on my window.

I KNOW YOU CALLED THE POLICE. YOU WILL BE THE THIRD PIGEON IF I FIND YOU DOING THAT AGAIN, OR TELLING ANYONE ELSE, INCLUDING YOUR BOYFRIEND.

I almost can't remember how I spent my time that evening. I failed to sleep. I examined my whole house to see if anyone had tried to break in, but I couldn't find anything. Maybe I should have felt lucky. Otherwise, I wouldn't even have the chance to tell you my story. I kept all the lights on. I fell asleep for a while, but not long.

Mike also noticed my unusual behaviour as he usually stayed at my place during weekends. But that weekend, I asked him to stay as long as he could. At first, he made fun of me for being clingy, but then he asked me if everything was okay. He was nice as usual, but I couldn't tell him the truth. He is the most important person in my life. I wouldn't take any risks with him. To my surprise, he turned serious after I insisted on him staying, which seemed like he realised there was something happening to me, but he didn't ask. I did wonder if he might also notice whether he was being watched by someone, especially when I remembered my stalker's message of "don't tell anyone, including your boyfriend". No way. If Mike did notice being watched, he would tell me immediately, because he was that type.

"You'll always have a strong guy there to protect you." He winked at me as he usually did.

The next day I phoned my sister via WhatsApp. My half-sister. The only other person who was mentioned by my stalker.

I never loved Rebecca. In other words, I hated her as soon as I began to remember things in my childhood. The reasons were straightforward. My parents only paid attention to her, without sharing any of their time with me. I heard my mother calling her "sweetie" and "my girl" all the time. For me, she might as well have forgotten my name, never even calling me "Liv". All the toys and books were for her, and never belonged to me. My parents always used the excuse that I was older than her, even though I was only a few months older. Apparently, kids are not stupid, even very young children. They're pretty sure about who gets more attention at home, and who is ignored. They take advantage of that all the time. She was that type, and she was also good at pretending to be a decent, considerate and brave person, because she knew our mother always had her back. All of these things enabled her to use every bad word with me.

However, I stopped caring about those things when I was seven, when she shouted at me, saying, "Everything here is mine, because Dad told me you're not his daughter."

Only then did I realise that I had never met my dad before, but I still didn't understand why my mother treated me unfairly. But it was good to know that, to make me not expect more.

When I was close to my fifteenth birthday, Rebecca was sent to the US by my parents to continue her studies. Of course, they didn't explain anything to me. I also didn't go to the airport when she left the UK, but I had her number in the US. My parents gave me her number and they told her to keep my number, just in case. Sometimes we greeted each other during Christmas, and we still met when she came back to the UK. But no more connection.

I didn't really care if I had her number or not back then, but now it seemed that this might have been the wisest decision my parents made. What did she say behind my back?

To my surprise, she accepted the call as soon as I dialled her number.

There were a few seconds of silence, which seemed like both of us were waiting for each other's voice first.

"What happened to Dad and Mum, Liv?" She was finally the first to break the ice.

"Huh?" I was frozen. "What do you mean?"

"Are our parents okay?"

"Yes," I said, "Why are you asking?" It seemed like both of us got confused by the conversation.

"Then... if they're good, why are you calling me?"

I felt the familiar tone, the one I could imagine in my mind as she looked at me suspiciously when she noticed that I got prizes at school.

Suddenly I was trying to restrain my fury inside. No, I needed to be calm. I needed the answer from her.

"Well, I have something else I would like to check with you," I said. "Did anything ever happen before you went to the US?"

"I don't know what you're talking about, you—"

"I'm being stalked," I interrupted her, "The stalker said you told him something about me."

"But I'm in the US now." I heard her slow wheezing. "It doesn't make sense."

"So, it seems like you know what you did," I said, "What the hell did you say about me?"

Silence again.

"Hello?"

"Yes, I'm here," she answered, "Well, I don't know if that's relevant."

"That's fine," I said, "I'm not here to blame you. I just want to know what happened. Look, I don't think I've brought trouble to myself before. The person who stalked me said I needed to pay the price for telling a lie. He mentioned you as well."

"Did he hurt you? Are you okay?"

"Not yet. But I don't know what he'll do next."

"Sorry. I apologise."

I couldn't believe my ears. This was the first time she said sorry to me.

"It happened during junior high school. Two boys lost their lives when they fought with each other, but I noticed the real reason was because one of them kept bullying another girl previously, so the other got into an argument with him. Then I told the police."

"That makes sense," I said, "But you were doing the right thing. Do you still remember their names?"

"Ummm… I remember they were called Mason and Tracy. Yes, I was telling the truth, but then I changed my words," she continued, "Other students didn't say anything. I was so surprised to see that no one was even trying to tell the truth. Nobody. Then our class teacher found me and asked me not to be a liar. He didn't even ask me what was going on. He told me that Tracy was always a good boy. I don't know why everyone was trying to maintain a good reputation for a bully, even if he had already paid the price."

"But then how could you relate all this to me?" I asked. To be honest, there was one second where

I was impressed by her courage to tell the truth before she continued.

"I got so scared when he said those things so seriously to me, so I said it was actually you who told me and I didn't see anything myself."

"And he believed you?" I asked.

"Do you remember the time when you picked up me from school when there was a heavy rain? Mum asked you to do that as she was busy at work."

"Yes, I was sick on that day."

"I told them you saw Tracy bullying that girl on that day when you were waiting for me." She had finally said the words I didn't want to hear. "I'm sorry, Liv. I didn't want to say that at first, I promise you. But I didn't want my class teacher and other classmates thinking badly of me. I didn't want to be isolated from the others."

***

To my surprise, my stalker stopped threatening me a few months after I called my sister. However, the feeling of being watched was there again after a while. I knew I was becoming more and more susceptible. Sometimes when I was walking in Oxford city centre, I tried to turn around suddenly to see if anyone looked like a stalker. But I found nothing.

After I contacted my sister, I still felt confused. I didn't think she was lying, but it was not likely the full story. According to what she told me, my stalker was likely a parent or friend of Tracy, who might feel furious about the news that I was trying to slander their beloved boy. However, it had been so many years, and what was the point in consistently stalking me, only to make me feel scared? There had to be other reasons.

It still bothered me all the time. One weekend, I told Mike, including the story my sister told me.

"You should have told me earlier about this, my love." He looked even more worried than me. "I feel bad for not noticing. At first when you asked me to stay longer, I thought it might have been because you watched horror movies or something."

He then stayed silent for a while, and suddenly he looked like he had decided what to do. "Let me think about how to help you."

"Don't call the police, because—"

"I know," he said. "That bastard must have already told you, and also, I don't trust the police. They're useless. I'll let you know when I have a plan."

"But I've never even seen the man before. How can you come up with a plan?"

"You're right, so I'll think about what we should do. I'll order a door jammer for you first," he said gently, but with a convinced tone, "Do you trust me?"

"Of course I do."

That evening was not as bad as I thought. At first, I was expecting him to not believe me or overreact. But neither were right. He was trying to solve the problem for me. We kissed and had sex, and I felt very, very happy.

***

I didn't see Mike in the morning. I was not surprised as sometimes he liked to go swimming in the gym in the morning, and he would come back by lunchtime. I usually sleep very heavily, so I didn't hear him getting up and making breakfast for me: scrambled eggs, avocado toast and grilled mushrooms. Sometimes I thought about our life together if we ever got married. We wouldn't stay away from each other anymore after he got a new job close to me. We would drive to work, make dinner and go travelling together. And soon

I would have a new family, one completely different from my original one.

Around 2 p.m. he was back with some Chinese takeaways and a small black handbag. Before I was about to ask what it was for, he sat down and began to talk.

"I worked out who's stalking you, Liv."

"Tell me you're not serious." I stared back at him. "How did you figure it out in just one week?"

"I have a friend who worked as a cop, and I asked him to check the CCTV footage from the past few weeks. There was a man. He always came up on the footage every time you were around. His name is Peter Wilson."

"We don't know him, do we?" I asked. "If your cop friend knows that it's him, why can't the police just arrest him?"

"No, we can't, Liv," he said, "First thing is that my friend is just doing me a favour. It may get him into trouble if we tell anyone about this. Also, look. This man hasn't done anything illegal. We don't have a lot of evidence to prove he has threatened you. You've already thrown away the notes he gave you, right?"

"Shit. They were so scary. I never thought about keeping them."

"Right. No, that's fine. But now you need to listen to everything I say, babe." He held my hand and met my eyes. "From now on, keep everything he sends you, no matter if it's a text message, a note, or even something else. Just keep it. Also, remember to put your door jammer on every evening. Don't open the door unless it's me."

"Okay." I had never seen him as serious as that moment. Then I noticed him taking out two phones from the black handbag.

"These are two burner phones. You take one and I take the other. From now on we only contact each other via the burner phones. They won't be able to be tracked. So, it's safer if I get more information from my friend. We won't know if that man also has a way to get access to your mobile phone. It's just in case."

I nodded. I never thought about that possibility. But he was right.

"Another thing..." He sighed. "We need to stop meeting each other until we get rid of that man. Sorry, Liv. But you'll be fine. I'll always be on the phone.

Contact me any time. You know I'm always there for you. What I do is all for your safety. I have a plan."

I wanted to say I didn't understand why we couldn't meet. Wasn't it safer if the man knew Mike was here with me?

But I didn't ask Mike. As he said, he had a plan. What I should do was trust. I always did. He had never disappointed me before.

"But I will miss you if you're not here." I lowered my head. "Every weekend I just wanna see you."

"It'll be over soon." He held me in his arms and kissed my hair. "I promise."

"You need to be careful," I said, "I don't want to bring trouble to you as well."

"Are you worried about me?" He winked and changed the topic. "Well, let's eat first. I ordered your favourite."

23

Joey

Something wakes me up during my nap after lunch at work.

Thanks to the small prayer room provided by my company, I can take a small nap and keep myself away from my colleagues. It always takes me a while to react when I'm woken up, but my phone then stops ringing. I pick it up to have a look. Unknown number. Just before I want to go back to sleep, a new email from the "tracking a person" website appears on my screen.

Shit. I forget that I had chosen the "call back" choice. But now I feel sick. I don't bother to call them back, so I click the email instead to have a look.

Dear Joey,

I hope this email finds you well. We tried to call you but we haven't heard from you yet. Here are the answers to some of the questions you had for us...

I quickly scroll down the page until the final line which talks about the cost.

Cost depends on the specific case. But can be from £1,500 for background checks and phone records…

That's a bit expensive for me as I don't have a lot of savings, and I'm not sure if it's worth doing. I do need more information from Olivia's previous records especially during high school. I'm not interested in her whole life. I did think about looking at her LinkedIn profile to see where her workplace is, but it seems like she hasn't updated it for a long time. Her most recent work experience was just an internship during her university days.

Suddenly, something hits my mind. I pick up my phone and dial Vinny's number.

He speaks as soon he accepts the call.

"Hey, you okay, love? Feeling bored at work?"

"Well, it's been sort of an exhausting day, Vinny. Just a quick one. Did Chris show you anything about Olivia Stretford's address or anything else related to her?"

"Nah, why? Don't tell me you're gonna follow her."

Fuck. This is exactly what I want to do. From the words Chris told me before, he felt sure Olivia was hiding something.

"Well, I know you, Joey. I'm not silly. But he hasn't shown me anything. And I don't think it's a good idea to ask him about the investigation."

"You're right. Fine."

"One sec." He suddenly stops me from hanging up. "I remember last time he told me there was a witness who claimed that he saw the dodgy man who was stalking her around her house on that day. He pretended he was a delivery man and knocked on her door. He showed me the CCTV video he had. But I think I can identify which street it was. But let me check if I'm right."

"Really?" I almost scream. "You never told me that before."

"You were already filled with too much information."

"Shit. I need to go back to work. The lunch break is over. Are you waiting for me when I finish?"

"I can't do that today as I might stay late at work. But tomorrow I can. You know I only need to work four days a week now. I won't let you be alone very often," he says, "If you still wanna track her, I will do that with you. Together. I know you care about that, but be safe, love."

24

Joey

It's almost 6:30 p.m. I dial Vinny's number again. Call failed.

Freaking hell. Vinny, please answer your phone. I'm sitting on the sofa on the ground floor of my workplace. I've called Vinny three times, but I get no call back from him. His WhatsApp status is still "last seen at 1:09". That's not like him.

I suddenly notice the red bar on my phone power indicator. Its power is running out after spending so much time waiting for Vinny. I grab my charger and find a socket to plug it in to. Or should I go home first and then leave him a message?

Olivia Stretford. The half-sister of the witness to my big brother's accident. Peter Wilson, her stalker, also the father of the possible bully. They do have connections. But it's not enough to produce a motivation for Peter Wilson's stalking, especially after so many years. Something is definitely off.

My thoughts are interrupted by the ringing of my phone. Vinny's number appears on my screen. Thank

God. I click "accept" and start complaining until I realise the person on the other side is not Vinny.

"Hello, this is JR Hospital. Is that Joey Palmer speaking? Vincent King was attacked by someone just now and he was sent to A&E. We noticed that you were the last person to contact him. Do you want to come here now?"

I almost drop my phone. I check my screen again to make sure it's definitely Vinny's number.

"What? Is he all right? When did it happen?"

"Half an hour ago," the man's voice continues, "He was hit by something heavy on the head and he's still unconscious. The police are here now as well. The detective says he knows you. So it would be great if you could come here."

I hang up the phone after I say yes. The detective knows me? That must be Chris. Freaking hell. I can't believe we're meeting again so soon. Suddenly a sense of guilt comes over me. Why and where was Vinny attacked? Was it related to what I was now looking for?

I don't have much time to stay in my mind. Luckily, I catch a taxi next to the train station. Half an hour later, a lane of pedestrians leads me to the entrance of the emergency department at JR Hospital.

To my surprise, Chris is already waiting for me.

"Hey, you okay?" he greets me, but he looks upset. "I told you not to keep tracking last time. But you didn't listen."

"How's Vinny?" I ignore his scolding. I've already blamed myself.

"He's still in surgery," he answers, showing the way to the waiting area near the operating theatre. "The doctor said his head injury was serious. And, Joey, to be honest, when I told you we had stopped the investigation... actually I was lying."

I give him a confused look.

"Three reasons," he continues without looking at me, "We do lack evidence, and we were tired of all the journalists and media. Also... I don't want you to put yourself in danger. I know you're a strong-willed girl, Joey. I'm sorry for what you've experienced recently and before. With my detective's instinct, I knew I needed to continue digging by myself."

"Are you telling me this because of Vinny?"

"I asked Laura to check the CCTV cameras," he explains, "It happened almost after 5 p.m. We don't know who the attacker was, but Vinny was there to follow Olivia."

"What?" I almost scream. No, Vinny. Why did you spend your work from home day doing this for me?

"I think the attacker was behind Vinny somewhere for a while, but of course, you wouldn't notice that if you were paying attention to something else."

"Were there any cameras which recorded what happened?" I ask.

"No." He gently sighs. "There were no cameras around there. I think the attacker deliberately chose a place without CCTV."

The doctor opens the operating theatre when I'm about to reply. He stares at both of us for a few seconds and tells us Vinny is fine now but still unconscious.

"We're not sure when he'll wake up. It won't be very soon unfortunately. He'll stay in hospital tonight."

Chris seems to realise what I'm thinking. "Go home now. I'll let you know when he's awake."

25

It's 12 a.m. Midnight.

Vincent opens his eyes. What he sees is darkness.

His hands are trying to grab something, but even he is not sure what he's looking for. Where is he now? He realises he is lying on a bed, but he smells something which does not belong to him. So, it's not his own place. His brain begins to dig through his memories, but a heavy headache suddenly fills his head completely. However, he is too weak to even scream. How terrible it is!

He can't remember when the headache finally disappears, but he can feel his body calming down. His eyes gradually get used to the dark around him. Everything becomes clearer. To his left and right are two small tables, but there is nothing on them except for a cup of water. His instinct tells him he is thirsty. But his memory is still stuck. He doesn't want to do anything until he figures out what's going on. Then he notices there is light coming from a tiny window just beyond the closed door.

Is this a hospital? The light outside is waking up his memory. He suddenly sits up in bed. Yes, he blacked out when he was walking in a small alley. Someone hit him on his head. That's why he has the headache. The memory keeps pushing forwards in his brain.

Now it all adds up. He had figured out where Olivia's place was from the CCTV footage Chris showed him before. As he'd been around there before with one of his friends, it didn't take him long to find out where her place was. At first, he was going to tell Joey, but he knew little about the truth of Olivia's supposed self-defence. What if Joey went to her place and got hurt? Instead, he decided to follow Olivia by himself to see how her life was and if she was meeting anyone.

He followed her in the morning and saw her walking into a big building just in front of a small cafe. He stayed there for the whole day and worked online on his laptop. During lunchtime, he noticed that she appeared outside the building. At first, he thought she was out for lunch, but then he noticed no one else was with her. She was just having a call, a long call, which lasted almost twenty minutes. Just after 5 p.m. he saw her leaving the building again.

He then left the cafe to follow her. He was not sure if she would realise someone was behind her, but he immediately pushed this concern aside, as she didn't even know him.

His memory went blank after that, just like someone took it away from his brain. He tried so many times, but he still couldn't remember when and where he blacked out. He only remembered he was supposed to pick Joey up from work and then go for dinner together.

Yes, he should message Joey now. She had to be concerned about him. Did she come here? He tries to sit up, but the sharp pain in his head begins again. Instead, his hands are trying to search for his mobile phone. After a few minutes, he retrieves it from his bag beside the bed.

Seven missed calls. Five unread messages. All of them are from Joey. No, one of them is from Chris, the latest one.

HEY, HOW ARE YOU FEELING NOW? CALL ME WHEN YOU WAKE UP. I'M AT THE HOSPITAL.

IS JOEY HERE? he types back. To his surprise, he gets a reply in a few seconds. There is a knock on the door, and he sees Chris standing there with a nurse.

"How are you feeling, sir?" the nurse gently asks, putting a stethoscope on his chest.

A few seconds later she nods with a relieved smile. After she tells Chris about his friend's physical condition and advises him not to spend too much time with him, she leaves the room.

It's Chris who breaks the silence first.

"Did you follow that woman by yourself?"

"Joey wants to know more about her," Vinny answers, "She believed there was a connection between Olivia's case and her brother, even her parents. It's good for her to know more about the past of her family."

"I knew it." Chris looks emotionless, but his worried eyes show everything. "You need to take care of yourself. Joey just came and she would like to see you, but I asked her to leave as it's late."

"Thank you." He's glad to hear that as he isn't willing to be seen like this. "But I wonder... why are you here?"

"I was around here to investigate another theft case, and then I noticed there were a lot of people accumulated in the street. I went there to ask and I found you. To be honest, I never stopped investigating the case, but I didn't want Joey to put herself in danger. But I forgot about you."

Vincent gives him an embarrassed smile, and then he asks, "So, should I tell her you're still on it?"

"No, I don't have much progress now. I'll let her know when I have something concrete in my hands," Chris says, "So, did you find anything unusual about Olivia?"

"Nothing too much, except for this afternoon," he says, "It might be nothing. I saw her leaving the building to make a call, but their workplace was on the second floor, and there was a rest place on the ground floor. If I were her, I would have just stood inside to make the call instead of going outside, especially when it was rainy. But I might be too sensitive."

"Umm, no, I think it's strange as well," Chris finally says. His flexible fingers are hitting each other. Vincent knows he does this when he's thinking. "Thanks for telling me. It's very useful."

Vincent is going to say something else, but he notices his friend has left the room after he tells him to look after himself.

26

Joey

Chris told me something before I left hospital. I've never thought anything bad about the people related to me, the people I stay with every day.

"Do you remember I told you not to tell your family anything about the case?" he had asked, sitting in the waiting area. "I think it's quite necessary for you to know."

He gave me a warning look and I was so nervous about what he would say next. He must have found something out, otherwise he wouldn't have talked like that.

"Last time, your cousin told you I went to your place to look for you, but actually I didn't."

"Why didn't you tell me this before?"

"I was busy with other cases." He crossed his legs, dropping his bag on the floor, "But I think it's strange, so I asked Laura to look up your family."

"You mean my aunt and uncle?"

"Your aunt is fine," he said, "She has her own company which she inherited from her father. But your uncle... he gambled a lot before, and he also worked at your aunt's company. And the records show he had a DNA test to check if he was Ava's biological dad."

"What? Then what was the result?"

"A zero percent match."

27

Olivia

Everything seems fine now, but Mike is being impatient with me these days. Also, there was a strange visitor at my house today.

She came to my place just after noon. At that moment I was about to text Mike and then I heard the doorbell ringing. Due to my previous experience, I didn't open the door immediately. Instead, I asked her who she was. After she claimed she was a cop, I finally opened the door.

The woman looked to be in her mid-thirties, with a slim shape in a black long-sleeved shirt and a pair of dark jeans. To be honest, she didn't look like a cop until she showed me her identity badge. Even though she looked very easy-going, I still looked at her with doubt as Mike's words appeared in my mind again: don't ignore the ability of the cops. Be careful all the time.

To be honest, I was worried because I didn't want Mike to be found out as he was the person who helped me, even though the method he used was illegal. Now

I need to protect him as well. If I didn't have him, I would still be dealing with the stalker.

She sat on the sofa opposite to me. When I was about to break the silence, she spoke first.

"So, nice to meet you. My name is Laura Williams. I'm Detective Bambos' colleague. May I call you Liv?" she asked.

I was frozen for a second when she was so straightforward, but then I reacted. "Yes, of course."

However, what she said next almost made me break out into a cold sweat.

"I'm here today as I need you to know something," she said calmly, "I hope you can leave your partner."

"How do you know I have a partner?" I jumped from my chair and asked her. I didn't realise my voice was trembling. I regret pretending that I knew nothing. But she was a cop. If she knew Mike was my boyfriend, didn't that mean she'd realise he killed that man, or think I got involved as well?

"I'm not here to arrest you or ask questions, Liv. I'm here to help you. I hope you can trust me."

"What do you know about us?" It was too ridiculous. I didn't even want to argue, but I needed to know how much she knew about us.

"Now I can't give you the answer," she said, "But what I can tell you now is that the detective is still investigating your case. I'm not sure how the process is going, but I know it's not your fault. And I don't think it's fair to see you get in trouble."

From these words I learnt three things.

The detective was investigating secretly. This woman was also exploring my life for a specific reason, and she might also know all about my stalker, even what Mike did. Otherwise, she wouldn't say I was innocent. Or they already had most of the evidence, and she was here to tempt me into telling the truth.

"I'm not here to make you confess anything." She looked at me firmly. Her voice was soft and calm, but still with a warning tone. "I'm not recording either. As I said, I'm here to help you. Of course, I know you won't trust me at first, but I need to let you know that your partner is a dangerous man. He's hiding secrets from you for a reason."

"Well, I don't know what you're talking about." I took a sip of tea. "You're a cop. If you know he's dangerous, why don't you arrest him instead of telling me?"

"Everything needs evidence, Liv." She sighed. "He might be involved in some previous cases. It's hard for me to track those in a short period of time. But I can promise you, I'm not lying."

She then stood up from the sofa after she left her calling card on my coffee table. "Here are my contact details. If you need to talk afterwards or if anything happens, contact me any time, even at midnight."

Before I responded to her, she'd already stepped outside my door.

28

Olivia

The woman hasn't made me change my mind about being with Mike, but if I have to be honest, I'd say Mike is too helpful sometimes. No matter what I say, he's always willing to solve the problem, instead of just saying some comforting words. Even when I complain about some of my stupid colleagues, he'll say something like, "Oh, they're awful. How can I help you with that?" or "Have you considered getting another job?" Then the next day he'll appear at my company to pick me up after work. He'll greet my colleagues, bring some snacks for them, and even say something like, "Treat my baby well." I feel good due to that sense of being protected, but sometimes I find myself relying on him.

On that day, I never expected him to kill that man in front of me and bring his body to my house without telling me in advance. All he said was, "Do what I ask you to do. You'll be fine."

After that day, the way I spoke to the police was all dictated by him. Everything did look perfect. I was never suspected as someone who might try to murder their stalker. The whole story was that he was trying to hurt me, and Mike never existed. I was just a poor victim, a well-employed, decent single woman. This was also the reason we began to use burner phones to avoid being tracked by the police. That's what Mike said. I always trusted him a hundred percent until that policewoman visited me. I have no idea how she knows all about us, the whole plan, maybe even the story behind my stalker. Until now, no one else came to my place or contacted me to ask questions related to the case. That means that woman, Laura Williams, as a cop, didn't report what she knows about us to the police.

So, does that mean maybe I should trust her?

No. I don't think so. If she didn't report what she should do, she's not a good cop that should be trusted. She must have her own reasons, own secrets.

This evening Mike calls me on the burner phone. To my surprise, he asks if we can meet at his place. He says he misses me too much. I ask if he's still worried about what happened before, but he seems relaxed.

"I think we're fine now."

For a second, I consider telling him about the strange woman. But the fact is I also miss him as we haven't really seen each other for about three months.

Life by myself after work each day is not fun. It's not because I'm still scared of being stalked. I don't have that feeling of being followed anymore. I'm just that type of person who's not able to stay on their own for a long time. I need company. I need the feeling of someone waiting for me when I get back home.

When we meet, he looks haggard and there's also scum on his chin.

"Are you okay, love?" I ask, trying to find some clues in his eyes. Bloodshot.

"No, just tired. But it's all fine after seeing you."

As soon as he begins to talk, I feel much more relaxed. It's still him. My handsome, brilliant man. He holds me tightly in his arms. His tongue is almost absorbing my whole body, as if I'm the only treasure for him. How could this man be dangerous? No way. I know he only wants to stay with me.

We talk a lot that evening.

"I would like us to have a baby," he says to me as we're going to sleep on the bed. "And he will sleep here between us."

29

Joey

When I get home it's already dinner time. No one else is at home. Ava told me yesterday that she was going on a date today. I'm not sure about Emily and Ethan. Maybe they went somewhere together. I have to admit that I don't think I can treat them the same as before after the talk with Chris. My cousin was lying to me, and my uncle might not be her real father. That's a big shock to me. Ava's lie doesn't make sense to me though. It seems like she's willing to have police around us. Does she know something? Are there more secrets amongst them? I'm not able to guess, but I feel guilty and corrupted. Vinny was trying to help me and now he's in hospital. Then I'm told the people I rely on the most might have some secrets. There's no one else I can talk to.

The house is empty. No one is cooking, cutting bread or making toast in the kitchen. The plates, forks and bowls are properly cleaned and set neatly to the side. Auntie Emily usually puts them in order. She never leaves them in a mess. There are also a few potted plants placed next to the window in the kitchen, owned by Uncle Ethan, but he always forgets to water them. They now look dry and lifeless. Recently I've been so busy with my life. Most of my time is spent on work and looking for ways to dig through the mysteries. I don't pay a lot of attention to my family. It seems like the first time I'm alone at home.

My attention turns from the kitchen to the bedrooms. The lights are all off. The doors are all half-open, leaving three dark holes for me. What secrets do they have? Please tell me you guys are not related to anything happening now or before. Suddenly I have a strong desire to have a look in their rooms. I know it's not proper to do that, but now it's not just my curiosity that pushes me. Chris' warning makes me feel unsafe. How else can I try to find out some clues? Maybe it's a great chance.

I walk into Emily and Ethan's big bedroom first. My instinct does not work very well now, but I don't want to go to Ava's room first, as I've always regarded her as my best friend. I tell her everything and she always treats me as her sibling. My sense of guilt starts when I think about going to her room, as if I'm trying to spy on a friend's secrets. Maybe her lying to me was just a coincidence. I'm not ready to face it at present.

The room gets rid of the darkness after I turn on the lights. The cupboard stands by the corner of the room, with a big paper box next to it. The cupboard is not separated by two halves, but I can easily identify which shelves belong to Aunt Emily, as she is an extremely tidy person. But both of them don't have a lot of stuff on the shelves, as if they are not staying here frequently, or maybe my room is too messy. Everything else looks more than normal.

Just then, I hear a key moving in the door lock. Shit. Someone's come back home now. No matter who it is, I'll need a lot of time to explain my creepy behaviour. What can I say? I also have to cross the living room connected to the main door if I want to go back to my room. Shit. I quickly turn off the light before the door opens. I may need to hide first.

"Joey. You home?" It's Ethan's voice. Is he alone?

My shoes. I didn't hide them. He must have realised I'm at home. Shit.

I don't have time to close the door of the bedroom. I try my best not to make any sound when I move under the bed. There's still some space. Then I hear his footsteps getting closer. I hear the sound of his bag dropping on the bed. His slippers are only one foot away from me. Luckily his footsteps move away from the bed and I hear the bathroom door close. After I make sure he is definitely in the bathroom, I slowly move myself from the bed and remove my slippers from my feet. I quietly walk cross the living room area in front of the bathroom and finally arrive at my own bedroom. Then I pretend I was sleeping and have just woken up.

"Hey, you're back, Uncle Ethan. Sorry, I was sleeping," I shout as I lie on the bed.

A few seconds later, the bathroom door opens. "Hopefully it wasn't me who woke you up." Ethan smiles at me. He looks as usual: approachable, calm and gentle. "Have you eaten?"

"Eh, no."

"Ava and your aunt won't be at home tonight," he says, "I'm gonna cook something and we can have dinner together. Tired?"

"Yes, I was exhausted at work today." I give a guilty blink. I'm not completely lying. "I might just sleep for a few more minutes. I had a few snacks at work so I'm not hungry. But enjoy your dinner."

"Huh? You sure?" He stops cutting the cucumbers and stares at me.

"Yeah," I say. Then I pretend to yawn to show how sleepy I am. Luckily, he looks convinced and then leaves me in my room.

PART THREE

30

It's Friday again. The weather is much better than a few days ago. The sunshine enters the room. Vincent closes his eyes to feel its warmth. It seems like he hasn't enjoyed the sun for a long time.

He hears the doctor's voice.

"Mr King, you're now good enough to leave the hospital. Please take care of yourself and don't do too many sports in the next few months." Then she gives him some other tips for further recovery and leaves the room.

He has already packed up everything. In other words, there is not much to do as he only has a small bag. He is more than ready to leave if he wants. It's been almost a week in the hospital. He's not been left alone though. Some of his colleagues brought lovely snacks and gifts for him, and Chris came to chat with him as well.

But where was Joey? He remembers he received a few missed calls from her on the day he got attacked, as he was supposed to pick her up after work. He did call back after he woke up, but all the calls went to voicemail. Finally, he received messages from her the next day. All of them were asking how he was feeling and when he would be allowed to be back home. That was it. Chris told him he'd updated Joey about everything concerning his injury, but he still feels a bit odd. He knows his partner. She prefers calls than cold messages. She talks a lot on the phone. She is caring, positive and sweet. So, it's odd that she's just leaving a few messages that could have been sent by anyone in his life. He thought she'd at least mention some stuff about Olivia, that lady she was concerned about. But she mentions nothing.

He did think about some possibilities. Maybe she feels guilty for making him go through this, and she doesn't know how to face him. Or maybe she was also threatened by someone and is now scared. He can't convince himself with either reason. It's just not like her. But now he can leave the hospital and find out himself. He is going to see her and ask her what's going on.

When he steps out of the hospital, he suddenly remembers a scene he once saw in a film. A man had just left prison and faced the strong sunshine that attacked his eyes. Now he feels something similar. No one likes hospitals, especially when there's someone he'd like to see immediately.

It's now around noon. She'll be working at present, but it's also around lunch break. That's the time she's usually on WhatsApp messaging him.

Around fifteen minutes later, he's downstairs in the building she works in with a Chinese takeaway, the one she always orders.

He tries to call her twice. No response. *She might have turned her sound off or she's not near her phone,* he thinks. This has happened before. Finally, he decides to go upstairs to find her. She works on the second floor. A young girl appears and opens the door for him.

"Hey, Vinny, you all right?" she says, "Are you here to find Joey? Unfortunately, she's not been here since last Friday."

"Oh, really? Do you know why she's off?" he asks.

"Umm... I heard her manager say she got a big cold recently. Didn't she tell you?" The girl looks a bit confused, then she continues with an evil smile. "Are you two not talking? Oh, come on. Joey is a lovely girl. Don't disappoint her."

"Uh, of course not. It's just because I'm super busy these days. Anyway, thank you, Georgia. Have a nice day!" He gives an embarrassed smile and stops the conversation.

Now he's more worried and confused. The last time he received Joey's messages was the day before yesterday. She didn't mention she had a cold. Of course, she also didn't say if she went to work. She didn't share much about her life. But she did ask when he would be discharged from hospital. And now she wasn't answering his calls and texts. What happened?

He has to go to her house to see if she's all right. Now.

Just then, his phone rings.

31

The call is not from Joey. It's Chris.

"Hey, mate." Chris speaks immediately after the call is connected. "How are you? Did you leave the hospital?"

"Yeah, I just left," he replies in a weak voice.

"Oh, that's a shame. I was thinking about grabbing you for lunch as I'm just around the corner from the hospital. By the way, you sound off. Are you all right?"

"Uh, I'm fine... it's just Joey is a bit weird these days. And now she's not answering my calls. I just went to her workplace, but her colleague told me she's been off sick from work since last Friday."

"Oh, I see." The detective sounds calm. "Have you checked if she's at home?"

"Not yet. I was going to and then you called me."

"Well, listen..." Chris' voice suddenly becomes serious. "I can't go with you as I have another case to work on at the moment. Jordan is with me as well. But I will ask Laura to go with you, just in case."

"Ah, thank you, but I think I'm okay going alone," he says sincerely, "I mean, you guys are always busy.

Joey might just be sick and not very willing to talk."

"Oh, come on." Chris changes back to his casual tone. "We're friends and I also think you need some sort of company. You know Laura. I completely trust her and she's also my other work partner. She always notices things we don't."

"Sounds good," Vinny replies.

"Where are you now then?"

"Just opposite the train station. There's an ice cream shop. I'm standing near there."

"Right," Chris says, "Laura will be there in ten minutes and you can go together. Tell me how it goes later."

"All right. Thank you, Chris," he replies and disconnects the call.

No more than ten minutes later, he sees Laura waving at him from her dark blue car.

"Hey." She winds down her car window. "Chris told me everything. Let's go and check her out."

"Thank you," he says and gets in the car, "Hopefully it doesn't bother you much."

"Oh, don't say that. Chris said you were his friend. I want to help as much as I can, especially when I saw that girl coming with you last time. She's gorgeous. We need to make sure she's safe."

He remembers Joey said she always needs to take the bus when she goes to work. It's around an eight-minute drive. To his surprise, Laura is not a serious type cop. Instead, she answers almost everything he asks. After some small talk, they come to the real topic.

"I think the fact I was attacked almost proves there's someone else related to Peter Wilson's death. What do you think?"

"That's for sure." Laura's voice turns cold. "That's why Chris asked me to come with you. Whoever that person is, he attacked you just because he wanted to warn you, but you were never his real target, Vincent."

"You mean, it's actually Joey?"

"I can't say so. But one thing's for sure. He and Olivia have connections. And he doesn't want others to know about it. Anyway, let's make sure Joey is safe first."

They arrive at Joey's house and ring the bell. The light is on. Then they hear footsteps getting close to the door. A female voice greets them.

"Hey, Vinny, we haven't seen you in a while." Emily looks happy when she sees him. She is always the more active type and she loves company. Then her smile turns to Laura. "Are you also Joey's friend?"

"Yes. My name's Laura. Nice to meet you."

Emily invites them into the house and pops to the kitchen. Ethan is sitting on the small sofa next to the kitchen reading. He nods and gives a welcome smile. However, they don't see Joey around.

"Joey's in her room," Ethan suddenly says, "Sorry. She's been sick these days, so she's not very chatty. But I'll ask her to come out and see you guys."

He stands up and walks towards Joey's room. He knocks on the door and goes in. Finally, they hear Joey talking inside. At that moment, both of them look at each other and feel relieved. At least she's safe.

"Sorry, we don't have coffee here. Is tea okay?" Just then Emily comes back with two cups of black tea.

"That's perfect. Thank you."

Both of them carefully put their cups on the table. Then they hear a familiar voice.

"Hey." Joey comes out from her bedroom with Ethan. She is wearing dark blue pyjamas with a pair of cotton slippers. Her voice is weak, but still clear. Her hair looks a bit messy too. She doesn't look surprised when she sees them, but Laura still catches something else. Something very off.

It's fear.

32

Vincent stares at Joey in the living room. He sees many emotions in her eyes: happiness, surprise and warning. Her dry lips move and try to say something, but she stops after she glances at her aunt and uncle. He feels a bit confused now he's made sure she's actually safe. Why does she suddenly treat him differently especially when he was injured at hospital?

"Hey, you're back, Vinny. How are you feeling now? I'm really worried about you." When his attention is fully on his girl, she comes over and hugs him. She hides her head in his chest, so he doesn't see the tears in her eyes.

Laura scans the house quickly. Nothing really looks suspicious. There is a small counter which is occupied with a lot of medicine close to the sofa. Apparently, the opened Lemsip capsules box is for Joey. Her aunt and uncle just walk back to their own bedroom instead of staying in the living room anymore.

"Shall we go to your room and talk?" Laura asks.

"Ur, yes, sure." Joey smiles and starts moving back to her bedroom, "It's so nice to see you again, Laura."

"Why are you not replying to my calls, love? I texted you as well," Vinny finally asks. He knows he might have been a bit impulsive deciding to follow Olivia without telling her. But the point is he would like to help her figure out what Olivia is trying to hide. It makes no sense that she would get upset over it.

"I'm sorry," she says, "My phone's been broken since yesterday." She notices her boyfriend looks much more relieved after she says that. That excuse will explain everything.

"Ah, that's why." He laughs. "Where is it now? Maybe I can have a look at it for you. I did it before."

Laura notices a flustered look in the girl's eyes after his words, but it disappears in a second.

"That's sweet, but I've already sent it to get repaired and then we'll see if it works."

"All right then." He looks relaxed. "Are you going back to work tomorrow?"

"I'm not sure. Maybe not. I mean, let's see how I feel tomorrow."

"It's not like my girl," he says, "You're the type that never wants to stop working. Are you sure you're fine?"

She gently nods and then smiles. "We all have a few days when we just wanna be with ourselves."

Then her attention shifts to Laura. She seems like she's trying to find the best way to start a conversation. They haven't seen each other since the day they came to tell the police about the weird messages she received.

Her behaviour is not expected by Laura. At first, she thought she would be so excited to have her boyfriend coming to see her, even if she wasn't feeling well. Also, she hasn't asked her for more information about Olivia's case, the one that she was working on with Chris. Is that because Chris has already told her everything? No way. Joey is a smart girl. There are suspicions all the time. Why were both Olivia and Peter related to her elder brother's death? It's too good to be a coincidence. Joey should have asked her about more details and any possible updates. But there's nothing from this girl.

Suddenly, Joey stands up and walks to her bookshelf. Her eyes don't stay on the shelf for even a second. It looks like she's already decided which book to choose. She picks a thin book with a colourful cover and brings it to both of them.

The title reads: *Stress Relief Book*.

"You know what?" She suddenly looks more relieved. "Vinny, do you remember I told you about a mental health session we had in my workplace?"

Vincent nods. "Yeah. But on that day, you were so tired and you didn't tell me what happened."

"Well, it's not something very special. It's just everyone had some nice food and a chat together. But everyone got this book. Look." She then opens the book. "There are so many amazing pictures with different words to colour in. It did make me feel good."

"How many pages are you colouring in?"

She begins to turn the pages. The first one they see is "Live. Laugh. Laugh."

Second page. "Stay positive."

"I really love this one. Look, I've almost finished them. I'll show you another two that I love."

Then she points out "Love yourself" and "I'm strong".

"Wonderful. I had a book like that," Laura says, "It really makes me feel good." After that, she stands up. "Right. Why don't I leave you guys here? It's time for me to go."

Joey's glance moves to Laura's face when she stands up. "Thank you for coming and checking on me. Sorry I'm a bit off these days. But I do appreciate it." Then she turns to Vincent. "Maybe you guys can go together. I'm not very chatty today. I just want to continue colouring in, especially my three favourites. I'll be fine in a few days. I promise."

"Okay, love." It's obvious that Vincent wants to stay longer with her, but he never expects to force her. "Let me know if you need anything, okay? You can borrow Ava's phone, can't you? Anyway, I'll go now."

Joey doesn't say anything but smiles. Then he gives her a quick kiss on her right cheek.

33

Ethan

I'm staring at my screen. The video clearly shows everything that happened in her room. I don't know who that girl is. Joey never mentioned her before. Anyway, they didn't talk about much. I'm happy that Joey is clever enough to not say anything about her current situation. She pretended everything was fine and she was safe. Actually, she is. I don't want to hurt her, but I can't allow her to find out all the secrets.

I'm not an evil person. I'm really not. I keep telling myself that, but now I've already done something bad. Very bad.

Everything started several years ago, when Joey and Joshua were only seven.

***

Maybe I shouldn't have come to the UK.

My parents divorced when I was very young. All I remember was the fighting between them almost every day because of the alimony from my father.

The way they looked at me was like they were paying attention to a product which could be used. Thanks to my grandparents, they supported me during university. They paid for my tuition and my other life expenses. I still remember what my grandpa told me: "Everything will be fine when you grow up, Ethan. Trust me. Get away from here."

I can't say if it was a comfort or an encouragement, but I could feel his words, his attitude towards me. It was totally different from my parents. It was deep love and hope. Even now I can feel their touching words somewhere in my heart which makes my eyes wet.

I told myself I couldn't disappoint them, and I studied so hard during university. I got scholarships every year, which provided me with the chance to be an exchange student in the UK for one year. This was a big change in my life. I can still remember my grandparents' faces when they found out.

That's my story before I came to the UK. I really wanted to make a big difference, to create a new future for myself. However, I lost my first job two years after my graduation due to a big redundancy in the company I worked for. It was a tough period for me. As I was holding a work visa, I didn't have a lot of time left to get another job before the date I had to leave the UK. I was feeling awful, without having a plan for the next step.

Everything was different after a careers fair. People always have more potential than they think, especially me, who was trying to impress the representatives from the different companies as much as I could. Then several days later, a senior member of an IT company contacted me and asked if I was happy to have an on-site interview as their CEO also went to that careers fair and he really liked me. I couldn't believe my ears.

The interview went pretty well. I also met the CEO. His name was Kevin, a well-shaped man in his late forties with ginger hair, and he asked me a few questions about my past experiences. To my surprise, he spent a lot of time praising my incredible efforts during my past study experiences, instead of being serious and unapproachable like some other leaders. Finally, I was offered a position as a data scientist, and my visa got sorted out again immediately.

I loved my job, as it was exactly my field. My focus was always on work until I saw a girl who worked closely with Kevin. After only one glance, I knew I was in love. Her age was close to mine, with similar ginger hair just like Kevin. She spoke gently. Her eyes crooked when she smiled. We also had a few connections at work, but not very many. At first, I thought she was his new secretary, but finally it turned out she was Kevin's daughter, Emily, when I expressed my feelings to her.

Our first date went really well. She was quite interested in my background.

"That's why Dad told me he hired a very talented young man recently. I'm impressed." That was her first comment about me. She also told me she would be the successor of the CEO position in the future.

Our relationship progressed surprisingly well. Kevin almost raised his hands in approval and regarded me as his son-in-law. I'd celebrated more than once how lucky I was as I gained both my dream career and love. We got married after two years. Some of my coworkers gossiped about why I approached Emily, saying it was because I was interested in the money. That was not true, but I didn't care anymore.

The turning point of our happiness arrived when both me and Emily wanted to try for a baby, but it was always silent in Emily's stomach. It didn't affect our relationship, but I could tell both of us were frustrated about it. Finally, one day I went to the hospital to check if I was infertile without telling Emily.

The answer was yes.

I was very depressed when I got the news. I didn't know how to tell Emily. I was also scared that she would divorce me if she knew the truth. However, just when I was ready to tell her, she said she had something to tell me too.

Then she took out a piece of paper from the hospital and asked me to read it.

"I'm pregnant," she said.

I didn't show Emily my diagnosis result. The timing was incredible.

There were a few seconds that I forgot about the infertility and I was really happy for her. I did love her. I knew she wanted a baby, and she was finally pregnant. But after that I spent a long time calming down and thinking things over. How was it possible? Was I just absolutely lucky or was it not my baby?

I still looked after Emily carefully when she was pregnant with the baby. I could feel my brain splitting into two halves. When I saw her gently touching her belly and talking to the baby, I told myself, "Come on, Ethan, it's your child. You're becoming a dad now. Why are you not happy?"

However, after she fell asleep every day just on my left side, I still failed to convince myself that it was my child. I once talked about this with one of my friends who was a doctor. He told me that it was still possible for an infertile male to make his partner pregnant, but of course there was less chance. I didn't think I was that lucky.

Sometimes she could see I looked worried. She always asked me if I was okay, with her big, blue innocent eyes. Two days after the due date, she gave birth to a baby girl. She named her Ava. We were too busy to pay attention to other stuff except for looking after the baby and having a lot of visitors. Kevin came and helped us a lot after Ava was seven months old, as both of us needed to go back to work after the maternity leave. Ava was very active and energetic. She looked like her mum very much, but she liked me. She always grabbed her toys and put them in front of me. I had to say I felt great during these moments, especially when she was using her little jelly hands to touch my cheek.

However, if she was my biological daughter, I would be a better dad.

I still held some hope before I asked for a DNA test between me and Ava without the permission of Emily, but the result hit me badly. It was very, very awful.

A zero percent match.

So I was right.

I really wanted to find Emily and throw this result in her face, but I still didn't. I was on a UK marriage visa now. If I divorced Emily, I would be sent back home before I could apply for a British passport. If that happened, all my efforts were in vain. My grandparents would be disappointed as well. Also, I still needed my job. I loved my job. I might not need it in the future, but I did need it now.

So I didn't say anything. I became more emotionless, but I acted like a normal husband, a good father and a hardworking worker. Sometimes I did want to ask Emily why she was cheating on me. Did she begin to pretend when she first met me? But what was the point? I didn't get the answer. I told myself not to care about this anymore. All I could do was wait until the day I was eligible to get permanent residence in the UK or a British passport.

I still overestimated myself. The slow burning furious emotion was gradually breaking me. I began to gamble to get some time just for myself. We started getting into quarrels, especially when she couldn't figure out where I spent our money, but I could always make up some good excuses and I was not feeling guilty. I was completely obsessed, until I lost loads of money one day. It was the worst loss I had. I had to find a solution.

I needed to get some money back, at least for now. Suddenly I thought about Emily's sister, Sarah. She helped us a lot during Emily's pregnancy as well, and she had twins, called Joshua and Joey after Ava was born. The kids got along with Ava very well. Both her and her husband, Oliver, looked like very nice people, and they both worked as doctors in the same hospital. If I asked them to get some money, I didn't think it would sound too bizarre.

I thought it was a very good idea, so I decided to go visit them after work. Their place was not too far from my workplace, so it wasn't hard to get there.

And then I rang the bell.

34

Ethan

There was still no answer after I rang the bell three times.

I felt frustrated but also confused, as it was almost dinner time. They usually preferred spending family time at home during dinner time. As it was still light outside, I couldn't clearly see if the lights were on or not. As I was about to leave, I suddenly heard something from the house. I didn't know what it was, but it was definitely from the house. I heard the sound for just one second, and then it was back to silence.

So they are in, I thought. *Why didn't they come and open the door for me?*

At first, I did want to just leave, but I tried to twist the door handle. To my surprise, the door was open.

There was darkness inside. No lights were on. I knew it wasn't polite to go into other people's houses without an invitation, but my curiosity led me in. There were some footsteps with mud next to the shoe cabinet at the door. I tried to call the name of my brother-in-law. Still silence. Then I heard another sound.

If I could travel back to the past, I would have just stopped and left.

But I didn't. I went straight in until I saw my sister-in-law's lifeless body on her back. Her head was almost completely covered in blood. Her arms fell to the same side as if she wanted to grab something. My brain was not working. I looked numbly towards the living room on my left side. Oliver was face down on the floor. He was a few steps away from me. I didn't dare get closer to see, but I clearly knew he was not breathing anymore. My instinct told me I should go immediately and call the police, but I moved myself past Sarah's body and to the bedroom next to her. I remember it was the twins' bedroom.

What I saw was something I will never forget. The door had completely collapsed, as if someone had forced it open and broke in. The little boy, Joshua, was curled up on the floor next to the couch with his back to me. There were bloody drag marks all over the floor. There were still some Peter Rabbit puzzle pieces scattered next to him. I didn't see the little girl, his sister Joey. I stepped back slowly and left the room.

To be honest, I had thought about calling the police then, but gambling had gone to my head. I knew that if I continued to be in debt to others, sooner or later Emily would find out everything. Then I would lose everything. An amazing job and the envious looks of people around me. I loved that feeling, even though my life was not perfect. But other people thought I was perfect. That was enough for me.

I'd been in their house before when Emily was pregnant, so I knew they always kept their cash, their bank cards and everything in the drawers of their bedroom. So I walked in and found loads of cash and some jewellery. I took it all without counting how much there was. After that, I left the house. I almost ran away. I kept running for a long time, as if there was someone chasing me. I couldn't remember how long I ran for.

I stopped until I saw a police station. I stood there for a few minutes, but I still wasn't ready to tell the police what I just saw. No, I couldn't. I would be regarded as a suspect, as I had stepped into the house without calling police immediately. I took almost all of the valuables. My fingerprints. Shit.

I finally calmed myself down after I had a cup of coffee. I didn't do it. There had to be more suspects other than me. It would be fine. My mind was trying to think about how the scene looked when I saw the bodies. More details were becoming clear. How their injuries looked and other details in the house.

Suddenly I remembered something strange.

I saw Sarah first. She was just lying in front of me. She'd lost a lot of blood. I even saw the blood flowing through the floor gaps to my feet.

But it shouldn't have been. Blood was thick and dried out very quickly. But her blood looked... fresh, as if the murder had just happened when I arrived.

I suddenly felt a chill on my back.

That meant the killer might have been still hiding somewhere in the house when I was there.

***

Sometimes we need to admit that our lives are filled with coincidences.

Just when I gave up on the idea of talking to the police and decided to head back home, I met Emily on my way back. She looked a bit worried.

"Today was the twins' birthday," she said, "Sarah told me to come to her house this evening and she would message me as we're having a party tonight. But she didn't answer any of my calls."

"Ah, I see," I said, trying my best to look innocent, "Maybe they were just busy with decorating the house or something else. Are you going now?"

She told me she was a bit worried as her sister was always a contactable person, so she would like to go and check.

"I'll go with you then," I said, grabbing my phone ready to call the police. It might be a good chance to call the police with my wife rather than alone.

I expected Emily's reaction when she saw what had happened inside. She was going crazy after she found out her sister was dead. At first, we couldn't find Joey, but the police finally found her in a suitcase under the bed, safe and without injury. When the police took her out and brought her in front of us, she was bending her knees with her arms and kept silent. She was not looking at anyone, not even crying. After Emily calmed down herself, she sat in the police station with a police officer who was sitting next to her and trying to comfort her.

"I'm sorry for your loss."

I failed to sleep that evening. I used to play with Joshua and Joey before when we visited their parents. They were just kids. Although I hated Emily, I didn't hate Ava, as kids are always innocent, such as myself in my childhood. They didn't deserve any violence or abuse. But Joshua was lying on the floor covered by blood when I saw him. Who the hell would do that to him? Now he was sent to the hospital. I hoped he was fine.

As both of her parents had died, Joey was sent back to our house. The police told us that we needed to take care of her from now on. The only thing that made me feel relaxed was that the police didn't have any suspects, and they regarded it as a planned robbery. Also, they found that the fatal injuries of both Oliver and Sarah were on their heads. The weapon seemed to be a small bamboo sculpture in their house, so they didn't pay too much attention to us except for asking some usual questions.

Me and Emily spent so much time talking with Joey, but she still stayed silent for a few days, except for sobbing in the evenings. We both knew how hard it would be for her, as she might have seen or heard how her parents and her brother got attacked. The police also came to us several times as they thought this little girl must have seen or heard something, but Emily asked them to leave. Emily treated her as her own child. She patiently coaxed her to sleep every day. After a few psychotherapy services provided by the police, she finally started to talk a few days later.

"It's all my fault. Will you catch the bad man?"

That was all she told the police. At the same time, the hospital updated us about her brother. He had a lot of operations and he was alive. But the doctor announced that he would have complications with his legs for the rest of his life.

Joshua was even more quiet than Joey after he left hospital, but he was very polite to us. He acted like a big boy. He tried to do the housework and look after his twin sister as much as he could. But I had a feeling he was always trying to hide from me.

These two kids then became a part of our life. Ava was feeling very sad about what they experienced, but she was also pleased to have her cousins living with her. She loved them even more than herself. As for me, I used the money I got from the house to pay off my debts from gambling. I was still feeling guilty, but I would keep it a secret. Yes, I was not a bad person. I just needed some money, and I didn't kill anyone. I raised their kids as well, so I didn't owe anyone money.

My only worry was the slight changes of the house when I went there with Emily, which validated my hypothesis. The killer was still there when I first arrived.

He might have seen me.

35

Ethan

Kevin, Emily's father, suddenly died of a heart attack after two years. After the funeral, Emily became the new CEO of the company.

This was the time things turned awkward. I didn't want to lose my job, as I was someone who didn't like many changes. I also had friends there. But I had to admit my wife had more power than me, and she cheated on me for many years. This feeling made me mad internally. I knew she probably had already realised she couldn't have a baby with me, but she never expected that I'd found out the diagnosis. However, she was an absolutely rich woman. That's how we could perfectly manage all the expenses after Joshua and Joey lived with us. I couldn't give up such a treasure like her. On the other hand, she wanted to keep me because I was talented with computers. I got an unusual promotion not long after I graduated.

I did all the housework at home, which always made her happy. Perhaps she also felt a little guilty for cheating on me. We were not like a normal couple, but a relationship with mutual benefits.

I was feeling empty until I met another woman, Olivia Stretford. Our first meeting was in a pub. Her phone was stolen there and she needed some help. Accidentally, we hit it off very well. She was sweet, elegant and made me feel protective. This was the feeling Emily could never give me, and I could feel that she also needed a man, like me, who could mentally support her.

We had dates very often, but she didn't know anything about Emily. I told her my name was Mike. We talked about everything. I could feel her sympathy when I told her my story about the reason why I came to the UK. I knew we had something common. Then she talked about herself, about being ignored by her family and half-sister.

Both of us were lonely, even if we were surrounded by many people every day. So, two lonely people came together and had a relationship.

I didn't feel guilty about having a relationship with her, as Emily cheated on me first. But I was always thinking about how to tell Olivia about Emily. I still haven't told her, as I'm afraid she will leave me because of my dishonesty. Actually, I'm an honest person, but I was scared to show the real me after Oliver and Sarah's case, as if someone was watching over me all the time. I even used my savings to rent a small apartment which was a bit far from my house, and I told Olivia to come there to see me when she was staying overnight.

I felt happier than before after I met Olivia, but I needed money too as always. Previous gambling always made me feel anxious about money. Maybe I could plan something to provide a better life for Liv. However, something else crashed in before I began to plan.

It was an evening during the school summer holidays. Joey went to Italy with her classmates. Suddenly, Joshua came to me after dinner.

"Uncle Ethan, I have something to talk to you about."

Joshua was sitting opposite me, legs pressed together with his fingers fiddling. I could tell he was struggling to say what he wanted to say. Finally he seemed like he was ready to talk.

"What's wrong, Joshua? We're always worried about you," I began, "To be honest, I'm happy that you'd like to talk to me."

And then what he said made me almost stop breathing.

"Why didn't you call the police at first?" He raised his head, with his cold eyes staring at me, full of sadness.

"What?" I couldn't believe my ears.

The dead memory was attacking me again. I didn't do anything except for taking all the valuables away. I came with Emily the second time. Then I pretended I knew nothing. Actually, I did know nothing. But how did he know I was there before?

"I was not completely unconscious," he continued, "My head was almost numb. Pain was everywhere. But I could still hear things. I heard the doorbell ring and you were calling my mum's name." He stopped, with tears on his cheeks, but he was controlling himself not to sob. "Why didn't you call the police at once? If you did, my mum... my parents might still be alive."

"I'm always sorry for your loss, Joshua." I never expected he was still conscious at that moment. "But I did call the police. Your aunt was coming to find you, and I came with her. We always feel lucky to have saved you and your sister at least."

"No. It's not like that. You did come first by yourself, and you didn't leave immediately. Then I couldn't remember anything. But I'm eighty percent sure it was you."

I shook my head and looked at him innocently, trying to convince him that it wasn't me. "Look, Joshua, you were badly injured and you couldn't move. Maybe it was just someone who sounded like me. Maybe that bad guy was still around you."

He didn't reply, just staring at me with a suspicious look. I relaxed a bit as he didn't have any evidence that that person was me. He didn't see me. It wasn't enough to judge only by sound.

"I expect you won't admit it," he said, "The reason why I didn't talk to you before was because I also doubted myself. But now I'm quite sure it was you. I want to know the truth. Why did you come and not call the police? I have reason to believe you were involved in my parents' deaths."

"It's not nice for you to say that, Joshua." I stood up and sighed. "Look, I have no reason to hurt your mum and dad. They were both good people. They helped us a lot when your aunt was pregnant with Ava. Now we're looking after you and your sister. I've never had any reason to hurt you."

"Well, I don't know. You know what you did," he said, "I should have just gone straight to the police, rather than talking to you. I hoped you would tell me the truth."

"But I didn't do anything bad. What would I tell?" As soon as he mentioned the police, I felt furious. I always thought it was my secret, but it wasn't. It was a time bomb.

"That's fine." He stood up with his crutches, willing to stop the conversation. "I will tell the police what I heard. If you left any fingerprints over there, it would be the evidence to match."

"One second." I finally made up my mind. "If you want to go to the police, I'll go with you."

He turned around and looked at me. He never expected I would say that.

"You won't believe me whatever I say, so maybe it's a good idea for us to go together. You always keep your sister safe, don't you?"

"What do you mean? She doesn't know anything about this. Are you threatening me?" He suddenly became nervous and stared at me angrily. "If you dare hurt her, there's nothing I won't do."

"Of course not." I stayed calm. "What about this Saturday? I'll go with you to the police station. We can tell them everything you heard. Then they're free to investigate me."

He narrowed his eyes, staying silent for a few seconds. "Ok." Then he left the room.

36

It's lunchtime on Friday. Joshua was alone at home, counting seconds. He would see his sister after she'd been to Italy for two weeks. Her flight should have landed now and she would come back soon with her classmate's parents.

He was also going to the police with Ethan tomorrow. When he spoke with Ethan last time, he recorded it secretly on his phone. He needed to be careful. He could feel his uncle was very dangerous. Now he had the recording, so if something happened to him, he would drop his phone and whoever found it would know what was going on.

He never regretted coming out from the wardrobe on that day. If he didn't, both of them might not be alive. He promised his mum to protect her. He never broke his promise, but there was never a moment when he didn't want to know the truth.

Suddenly, his phone rang. An unknown number. But he still picked it up.

"Hello," he answered emotionlessly.

"Joshua, where are you now?" Ethan's anxious voice came from the other side of the phone, "You need to come to the hospital, now! Joey got into a car accident."

"What? What's going on?" There was a second that he doubted what Ethan said, but his tone didn't sound fake. He clearly knew his uncle might be hiding something, but he had no motive to hurt his sister.

"Their car was hit by another van on the busy road around the nearby park. All of them were badly injured. I'm still waiting for news from the doctors. But you'd better come as well. My phone's dead and I borrowed someone else's." Joshua also heard a lot of background noise from the hospital.

His mind went blank, and he had almost no time to think. He quickly hung up the phone and rushed out of the house.

Please. Please be okay. He really couldn't accept anything happening to Joey.

Thirteen minutes later, he met Ethan in the hospital. He hugged Joshua at once.

"Don't worry." Ethan looked relieved. "They're all fine now. The operation was successful. Your aunt is over there with them. Let's go together. Your sister's room is the first one from the end of the corridor. I'll quickly go to the bathroom, but I'll be with you very soon." He put his arm around Joshua's shoulder and left in the opposite direction.

Joshua almost rushed to the ward at the end of the corridor, but he saw no one inside when he reached the doorway. The ward also didn't look like someone had just been in there. The lamp emitted a faint light.

Just when he was stunned and confused, someone covered his mouth and nose from behind with a wet towel. He didn't have time to react.

Half an hour later, a violent noise alarmed loads of people near the hospital. A man pushed his way into the crowd and asked those around him what was going on.

"A boy fell from the hospital rooftop. It's horrible. He is still so young."

More and more people joined the crowd. Some of them began to call the police. Shortly, the police arrived and dispersed the crowded.

The scene was so chaotic before the police arrived that no one even noticed that a hand in the crowd took away the mobile phone that fell next to the boy's body.

37

Ethan

That evening was a second nightmare for Joey.

All of us were sent to the police station to identify if the body was Joshua Palmer. Joey's eyes were numb. She stared at her brother's sneakers and stayed silent. She refused to admit it was her brother. Finally, Emily and I followed the police routine records and confirmed Joshua's identity. The policeman who was with us showed much sympathy to us.

"Poor kid. She lost her whole family. I couldn't imagine."

I'm deeply sorry, Joey.

I was sure Joshua hadn't told her anything about me, otherwise my life wouldn't be so calm. Joey was not the same as her brother. She was very impulsive and emotional. Joshua was never impulsive unless something happened to his sister. And I took advantage of this. To be honest, if he were my son, I would love him very much, but I wouldn't allow anyone to break my life.

It was his fault that he knew my secret. Not mine. I would take care of his sister for him. I promise.

But my life didn't calm down after all. Although the police claimed that Joshua's death was an accident, there was one thing that made them feel awkward. They couldn't find his mobile phone to get any extra information. I found it weird too, as I didn't take it. It was impossible for him to leave it at home as he needed it when he went to the hospital to find me. My instinct told me something was off.

And I was right.

A few days later, I suddenly received a message from an unknown number.

HEY, GUESS WHAT I FOUND ON YOUR NEPHEW'S PHONE. HE WASN'T THE ONLY PERSON WHO KNEW. I WAS SO LUCKY YOU DIDN'T SEE ME IN THE WARDROBE.

When I saw the message, my hands were shaking heavily. They seemed to know so much. The sender had to be the murderer of Joey's parents, and he was still in the house when I arrived. Also, he knew I killed Joshua in the hospital.

He almost knew everything about me. He was watching over me all the time.

But who was this person?

Before I replied, a recording was sent. When I pressed the "play" button, both Joshua's and my voice came out. It was that evening when Joshua came to find me!

Shit. He recorded it.

WHAT DO YOU WANT? I typed.

The reply came in almost a few seconds.

YOU ARE A CLEVER MAN, ETHAN. DON'T WORRY. I WILL KEEP YOUR SECRET AS WE ARE TWO GRASSHOPPERS ON THE ROPE. BUT YOU KNOW WHAT I WANT, DON'T YOU? TOMORROW AT NOON BRING £1,000 IN CASH TO THE TELEPHONE BOOTH NEXT TO OXFORD STATION. AS SOON AS YOU DROP IF OFF, LEAVE IMMEDIATELY. IT'S NOT TOO MUCH MONEY FOR YOU, IS IT? YOU CAN AFFORD TO RENT A PLACE FOR YOUR GIRLFRIEND AFTER ALL. AM I RIGHT? I BELIEVE YOU WON'T CALL THE POLICE.

38

Stay positive. Love yourself. I'm strong.

These words keep jumping into Laura's mind as she's driving back. She feels it was so random for Joey to mention these, as if she mentioned them for a reason. She's not quite sure if Vincent noticed it as well.

Her phone rings after she parks her car. It's Chris.

"Hi, did you guys check it out? Is she good?"

"Umm yes, she's just been feeling sick these days." She doesn't tell him about the odd behaviour. "That's why she didn't go to work."

"Okay. That's good."

They talk some more then hang up the phone. Laura then dials Vincent's number. There is something on her mind, but she needs to double check.

"Hi, may I quickly ask you about something? Does Joey like playing coding games or puzzle books?"

"Puzzle books?"

"Yes, well, in other words, games that give you some hints or clues and ask you to decipher the code..." Even she thinks her guess is a bit too bold, but she trusts her instinct.

"One second. Oh yes, I get what you mean." His voice turns into excitement. "Oh my God, she loves them so much. She was so obsessed with them. I remember the last time she showed me one. It was about a phone keyboard. You had one to nine, and other letters on the phone keyboard, so if I say one-two, that means the second letter on the 'one' button. Something like that. Not sure if it helps you."

"Ok, I see." She sighs, feeling a bit disappointed. Joey didn't mention anything about numbers. Maybe she's just overthinking things.

"Is there something wrong with Joey?" Vincent asks.

"Well, I'm not quite sure," she answers, "Did you find anything unusual about Joey today? I mean, I feel it was a bit random for her to talk about the mental health book."

"Umm, I think she's fine, just tired." His tone is uncertain. "Her personality is like that, and she loves some weird stuff, like the book she showed us today. I can see she's tired and not in her best mood. But to be honest, I feel the way she replies to my messages is a bit different compared to before."

"How different?" This piques her interest. Now anything matters.

"I'll show you some chat history between us. You can have a look. Her replies are very short and not as casual as before."

"That would be great. Thank you, Vinny," she answers and disconnects the call.

Vincent sends a few screenshots to her phone. There are also date marks on the chat, so it's clear to identify when it was.

The first few screenshots are from the dates before Vincent stayed in the hospital. Laura pays attention to the white boxes on the left side.

NOT BAD THEN. IT'S A BIT BUSY TODAY BUT EVERYONE IS SO DRAMATIC LOOOL. TODAY ASH MADE A FUNNY EMOJI OF ME AND SENT IT TO EVERYONE LOL. I'LL SHOW YOU.

Then the last screenshot is from two days ago.

I'M SORRY, VINNY. I'M NOT FEELING VERY WELL THESE DAYS. SO I DIDN'T REPLY MUCH HAHA. BUT LET ME KNOW WHEN YOU LEAVE THE HOSPITAL. I MISS YOU SO MUCH XX.

It's clearly two people who are replying, she thinks. It makes sense why they didn't see her phone earlier. Someone must have taken her phone and was now replying to her messages.

And there must be something else hidden from the way she talked about the mental health book. But Laura can't find any numbers related to it.

One second. She tries to remember what Joey had said about the pictures and sayings.

"This is my first favourite... Umm and then this one... and that one as well."

One. Two. Three.

Her phone rings again.

"Shit," she says, as she hates people disturbing her when she's thinking. But she still picks up the phone.

"Hey, I think we found something else in Peter's house. We're sorry we didn't notice it before."

39

Olivia is sitting downstairs in the hotel lobby. Her eyes are distracted and no longer look energetic. After she checks her watch and makes sure no one is paying attention to her, she stands up and takes the lift on the other side of the lobby.

Room 1203.

She takes her access card out. No one is in the room now.

Of course, she thinks. *It's still early.* She then lies down on the white bed and closes her eyes. Her heavy breath never cools down. They used to book hotels like this sometimes before. But now everything is different. A strong fatigue comes to her in a few minutes, which leads her to sleep.

She doesn't know how long it's been until she hears someone knocking at the door.

Her boyfriend is facing her.

"What's wrong, Liv? Who told you?" He looks anxious, with a pair of dark eyes staring at her. This is the first time that he makes her feel uncomfortable.

"I need to call you Ethan from now on," she replies emotionlessly, "I feel so silly for being cheated on all this time."

"No, it's not what you think." He steps forwards to take her hands. "I can explain everything."

"What can you explain? Are you going to talk about how you killed your nephew? Or are you going to explain how you were blackmailed by my stalker?"

He looks at her in shock.

"No! Tell me! Liv, who told you these things?" he roars loudly, grabbing her shoulder tightly. "You need to be on my side. You can't betray me!"

"I never betrayed you. It was you that ruined all of this." She stares straight into his eyes. "I can't believe I ever wanted to marry you. Now I just need the truth. Did you do those things?"

"Yes, I did!" he screams. "I killed that boy. It's all his fault. Why did he force my hand? If it wasn't for him, I wouldn't have been blackmailed." He pauses, then quickly grabs her neck. "What else do you know, huh?"

Her face turns red immediately followed by slight coughs, but he has no intention of letting her go. Just then, there is a sharp pain in his back, which makes him loosen his hands.

"It's you! How could you..."

Laura is facing him, with another man pointing the gun at his head. Joey is standing aside with tears in her eyes.

"It's disappointment for you, Mr Johnson." As she is saying this, the man quickly puts handcuffs on his wrists, "You are arrested for the murder of Joshua Palmer and Peter Wilson."

"You were already hiding here before I arrived, weren't you?" he asked.

"Correct," Laura replies. "After I got Joshua's phone from Peter Wilson's house, I figured out everything about you and Liv. I think you may also be a bit confused why Peter was threatening Liv, because you thought his target was you, but actually both of you were his targets."

Ethan gives her a confused look.

"Peter's son, Tracy, died several years before due to an accident with Joey's big brother. Liv's sister was also his classmate, but she told everyone that Liv was the actual person who claimed Tracy was the school bully. Peter couldn't accept someone talking about his son like that, even if it was true. Although we didn't have enough evidence to prove Peter killed Joey's parents, he had a sufficient motive. And you were the first one to arrive at the scene without calling the police, and that's why you were blackmailed by him."

Ethan is fully stunned. He looks at Joey, then at Olivia viciously. "You already knew the reason why he was doing this to you, didn't you?"

"What should I have done? It was you who told me you would sort this out for me. I always trusted you, then what happened next? You came to my place that morning and brought a box with his body. You told me to follow what you said then both of us would be fine. Actually, when he was blackmailing you, you just used the idea of protecting me as an excuse to kill him, and then let me admit that I had accidently killed him in self-defence. That way, even if the police looked into the case, they would only focus on me as we were using burner phones to contact all the time!"

"Then how did you know my real name was not Mike?" he asks.

"Because Laura came to my house and showed me the recording between you and the poor boy, you bastard," she answers with tears, "Of course I identified your voice. It's both familiar and strange to me..."

He suddenly laughs loudly, as if he didn't get involved in all of those cases. Then he pays attention to Joey.

"How did you find her?"

"We've monitored you for a while," Laura says, "And we saw you put her in the car trunk. By the way, thanks to Joey's secret messages, I realised she needed help. 'Stay positive. Love yourself. I'm strong.' If you pick the first, second and third letter of these three phrases by order, that would be SOS. As long as the car was parked, we could rescue her out of the car. By the way, I guess you began to keep her at home without her phone because she nearly found out your secrets."

"Of course she did, like her brother. They would be fine if they didn't dig around." He gives Joey a provocative look. "I don't know why she was focusing on Olivia, and even asked Vincent to follow her. I couldn't allow her to find out about the relationship between me and Olivia. I saw her searching my room from the home surveillance, so of course I couldn't let her go."

"So, that's why you hurt Vinny?" says Joey. "You always think it's other's fault, but you did all of this! Give Joshua back to me!" Joey finally can't help but break down, using her knees to cover her tearing eyes.

Olivia stands up, walks to her side and hugs her gently.

Ethan doesn't even look at the girl but turns to Laura. "Well, you explained everything. Take me away."

Laura waves to the man next to her, and they open the door.

Then they see Chris smiling at them outside.

40

"Why did you ask me to come with you? Everything okay?" Laura is looking around the corridor of the hotel.

Chris leans on the railing, standing opposite to her.

"Where's Joey?" she asks.

"I've asked Jordan to send her back home. Don't worry." Chris smiles. "So, it seems like you've solved this case, haven't you?"

Laura gently nods. "Sorry I didn't let you know. I wasn't sure at first."

"No, that's not a problem at all, Laura," he says, as his face turns dark. "No, I need to call you Ellie."

She puts away her smile and slowly raises her eyes to face him. Seconds of silence. Then she smiles again.

"Nothing can be left uncovered if you're on it, Chris. I knew it would finally come to me."

He takes out his mobile phone, scrolls for a few seconds and passes it to her. It's a picture of a teenage girl. She looks sweet with her dark hair and brown eyes, but a lot of red rashes are quite obvious on her face. A name is noted clearly under the photo: Ellie Lambert.

"To be honest, I didn't notice this at first when I was reading the yearbook, as you're too different now." He stares at her ginger hair. "But I noticed when I heard you mention Lucas was Rebecca's class teacher. Look, I only asked you to check on Rebecca, so at no point could you have known this piece of information even if you worked out Lucas worked in that high school as well."

"I'll never forget him. He was not my class teacher. He was a monster," Ellie says in a cold tone, "Death is not enough for him. Well, it's true that Tracy bullied me all the time. He cut off my hair, overturned my desk, verbally insulted me every day, and even locked me in the toilet on purpose. And you know what? Lucas was just watching all of this happen. He didn't stop him. There was even a time when Tracy said I was a gorilla, and he was standing there, laughing heavily."

"I'm sorry to hear what you experienced, Ellie." Chris holds her trembling hand. "But what you did, Ellie, wasn't worth it. He wouldn't have realised he was hurting you, but you killed him and ruined your own life."

"You don't have any right to say that to me, because you weren't me." She bites her lip almost to bleeding with her face full of sadness. Her chest is uncontrollably trembling, "No one had my back, except for Mason. But I can't believe he fought with Tracy and they both..."

"Then what happened next?"

Ellie shows a sad smile. "Well, we both work as police. You know the process. Journalists were trying to get as many answers as they wanted, and Lucas, that asshole, was telling them it was all Mason's fault and he was asking the whole class to say this too. And then another girl, Rebecca, was on Mason's side and she spoke the truth. But finally, she didn't dare to anymore. Poor Olivia. By the way, afterwards I heard that Tracy's father always secretly gave Lucas money to ask him to take good care of Tracy, and that's why he was so ridiculous."

"But I still have one thing that I don't understand, Ellie," Chris says, "Did you plan to end Lucas' life?"

"No, of course I didn't. Do you remember the day you interviewed him? I went to visit him in the evening, as I wanted to see how he would react when he saw a completely different me. When he opened his door, he was drinking beer and didn't realise who I was. When I finally told him, he was really surprised and then he giggled. 'Oh, I can't believe that's you. Well, actually if you looked like this before, I don't think that little shit would have bullied you like that. If I was him, maybe I would do that too.' After he said that, he just laughed as if he'd heard something really funny. At that moment I just felt there was something warm in my head and I shot him."

"I always want to say I loved working with you. You're able, smart and a kind person. I never knew what you experienced before. I'm so sorry." Chris lowers his head. "But I'm a detective. Today will be the saddest day of my career."

She raises her arms flat. "Go on then. I know it's the end."

He stares at his handcuffs and there are a few seconds where he hesitates. "No, it's not. You just made a mistake, but there'll be a new start for you. I promise."

She raises her head and meets his sincere warm eyes. For a moment, she feels that this man is not a detective, but the person she had dreamt of most in high school, the one that really supported her.

But it's too late.

4I

It's a Saturday morning. Joey and Ava are sitting in the garden enjoying the sunshine.

"What did you say just now?" Ava has a sip of her tea and smiles at her cousin.

"I said I've got enough deposit to rent a studio just for myself," Joey replies, "I'm thinking when to move out."

"Are you? I'm so happy for you." Ava looks excited. She even sits up straight, but she turns serious. "Actually I want to as well. Maybe we can move out together."

"Are you still upset about your parents?"

"I don't know." Ava shrugs slowly. "I just feel a bit awkward if I continue staying in this house, especially when I know my father is not my biological father and he did something bad, especially to Joshua. I'll never forgive him."

"You look like you already suspected him."

"Do you remember those unknown messages?" Ava suddenly asks.

"Wait... that was you?" Joey had still been thinking about those messages yesterday, and now she has the answer. She looks at her cousin in surprise. She never expected it to be her.

"I always wanted say sorry to you for making you confused." Ava avoids eye contact with Joey. "I know you wanted to know what happened to Joshua. One midnight I got up to go to the toilet, and I heard Ethan on the phone. Of course, I didn't know who it was, but I heard him say, 'It's too much', 'He heard me when his parents died' and 'I know you did it'. The first thing I thought about was Joshua. And then you know what? The next day, after you and my mum left home, he suddenly asked me why I got up during the night. He looked like he was concerned about me, but the way he asked me was very scary, and he still looked at me suspiciously even when I said I went to the toilet."

"My God." Joey is frozen. "So, that's why you sent me those messages?"

"At first, I just wanted to tell you straight, but the thing is I noticed he was watching over me when I was at home. I should have just texted you what I heard, but I was also scared, as you were sometimes impulsive. I didn't know what he would do to you if you went and asked him."

She stops for a few seconds.

"That's why last time when I texted, I asked you to call the police if I didn't come to the cafe as I just wanted to attract their attention to Joshua's old case, or even your parents'. I even lied to that detective to attract his attention to this house. I expected them to question me and then I could tell them what I heard. It sounds ridiculous, but I just wanted to use this as something you could use to get help from the police. Then I couldn't believe my messages also got involved in your big brother's case and they had connections as well."

"Actually, I understand." Joey purses her lip. "I guess you didn't call the police yourself because you didn't want to accept that your father was guilty."

"Yeah... I think so. I still can't believe what he did to Joshua." Her disappointed face looks so heartbreaking. "Your brother just wanted the truth. I can't imagine what Ethan would have done if you had asked him."

"Both you and Joshua know me so well. Actually, yes, I guess if you told me, I would have gone and asked him, like Joshua did. Then I would have been murdered too."

"My God. Don't say that." Ava still wants to say something else, but she finally gives up.

Joey slowly takes out her phone and shows a photo to Ava. This photo is a screenshot from Joshua's mobile phone found in Peter Wilson's workplace. It seems like a note.

"Ava, I really wish he was still here."

TO WHOM IT MAY CONCERN,

MY NAME IS JOSHUA PALMER. IT'S ALMOST MY SIXTEENTH BIRTHDAY. IF YOU'RE READING THIS, THAT MEANS I'M DEAD.

MY MUM IS SARAH JONES AND MY DAD'S NAME IS OLIVER PALMER. THEY WERE KILLED NINE YEARS AGO, AND I DON'T KNOW WHO ACTUALLY DID IT. MY UNCLE IS ETHAN JOHNSON. HE WAS THE FIRST ONE TO ARRIVE AT THE SCENE BUT HE DIDN'T CALL THE POLICE. I'M NOT SURE HOW MUCH HE IS INVOLVED IN MY PARENTS' CASE, BUT I FEEL MY LIFE IS IN DANGER AS ONLY I KNOW HE IS LYING. IF YOU SEE HIM, PLEASE, PLEASE CALL THE POLICE AND MAKE HIM TELL THE WHOLE TRUTH! I HOPE HE IS NOT SUCH A BAD PERSON BECAUSE MY COUSIN, AVA, IS A GOOD GIRL. SHE IS MY FRIEND. I MISS MUM AND DAD EVERY DAY. I WANT THEM TO HUG ME.

I HAVE A TWIN SISTER AS WELL. SHE IS THE ONLY
PERSON WHO MAKES ME SMILE NOW. HER NAME IS
JOEY. I LOVE HER VERY MUCH. MUM ALWAYS ASKED ME
TO PROTECT HER. I THINK I DID IT WELL, BUT I FAILED
TO SEE HER GROW UP AS AN ADULT. I HOPE SHE
WILL MOVE ON IN HER NEW LIFE, FIND AN AWESOME
PARTNER TO PROTECT HER AND BE SAFE AND HEALTHY
ALL THE TIME. IF YOU SEE HER, PLEASE TELL HER I'M
SORRY I DIDN'T TELL HER I HEARD ETHAN ON THAT
DAY. I'M SORRY I CAN'T PROTECT HER ANYMORE. TELL
HER SHE WILL ALWAYS HAVE MY BLESSING, AS WELL
AS MUM AND DAD. WE WILL TURN INTO STARS TO
PROTECT HER FOREVER.

JOSHUA PALMER

Milton Keynes UK
Ingram Content Group UK Ltd.
UKHW011822020224
437173UK00006B/13